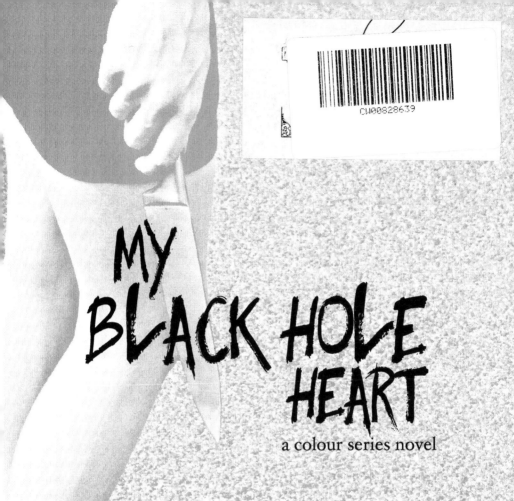

MY BLACK HOLE HEART

a colour series novel

A. GIANNOCCARO

For Rick,
This year was hard, but together we made it to the end.
Your strength inspires me.
Your support keeps me going and your love makes every single day worth it.
I am not me without you.

xx

ACKNOWLEDGEMENTS

Every book takes a small army to get it from inside my head and onto the pages, this one was no different. 2015 was filled with some epic highs for me and some very hard lows and my little book tribe was with me through both of those. I had a number one book on Amazon with Mary, something I still can't believe. Thank you, Mary for bringing The Goodbye Man to me. A little dream became a huge reality for me. When I wrote my first book I told myself, 'I can do anything,' and I have done just that.

I spent weeks sitting beside my husband in a hospital bed after an accident that could have easily taken him from me and my little girls. I have so much to be thankful for, don't take life for granted, tomorrow is never promised.

To my friends and family who were there to hold me up when I was down, thank you. I am not entirely sure how I would have managed this one without you. Mom and Dad for saving me in little ways that meant the world—thank you. Rick's Mom, Dad and Nana, Kelly, Ian Gianni and Ang for sitting with Rick while he was healing so I could get these words on the pages thank you, I cannot explain what it meant to have all of your support when we needed it so much.

To my street team Ashleigh's Assassins. You ladies are amazing, we may be a small bunch we are a special one. Thank you ladies for sharing, posting and helping me promote my stories, I appreciate every single post.

My Beta's, Michelle McGinty, Di Covey and Tracy, thank you, you read the word vomit and listen to my stupid worries, your honesty and time are something I cannot work without. Michelle, a special thank you for reading it in bits as I went, this was something I needed so much.

My editor, beta and book person Karen Mandeville-Steer. What would I do without you? Thank you for being the voice of reason, the kick in the butt and the one I can always rely on. You are a very special lady.

My sister in law Kelly Douglas. Your pictures are art and I am honoured to have one on my cover, thank you for trespassing with me to make my cover vision a reality.

Ciara Giannoccaro, thank you for being so beautiful inside and out, you made the perfect Avery.

Cassy Roop from Pink Ink Designs, you turn my ideas into reality and make my books beautiful. You are the best, I cannot thank you enough every time I work with you, I am blown away.

To the book bloggers, groups and promoters out there thank you. Without you, I would never have been seen and my dreams couldn't have come true without people like you. I know sometimes it's a thankless job and I want you to know that I thank you.

Twisted Sisters Blog and Group. What can I say except I feel like we all really are sisters, you are the place where my wicked mind feels at home.

To my readers, this was so bittersweet for me, I have come to love these characters so much and ending their story wasn't easy. I hope I have given you an ending that will be loved as much as the beginning. I thank every one of you for investing your time in my stories and for loving the characters like I do. Without you I couldn't do this.

WARNING

I write dark stories about things that will offend many people, but if you take the time to see through the darkness, you will find the stars shining in it. Life is not always happy, or easy, or fun—sometimes it's really hard.

This story contains themes that may be triggers or upset sensitive readers. I don't ever promise happily ever after because I tell stories about people who are not always looking for them. You have been warned, I am not responsible for tears, therapy or Kindles that are hurled across the room.

xx

Note

I write in British / South African English so some spelling, pronunciations and grammar may differ from American English.

MY BLACK HOLE HEART

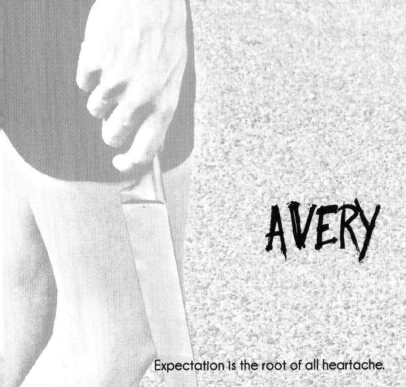

AVERY

Expectation is the root of all heartache.

I AM A KILLER. I have been since I was fifteen. My young girl hands curled around the handle of a knife as I filleted a man, his screams are etched into my mind forever. Sticky blood coated my fingers with every slice I made through his flesh. I knew long before that what life had in wait for me, so I never tried to change it. I was born to be a killer. I didn't choose it, it chose me. I have a black hole heart that beats nothing but the blood of others.

The saying goes—it takes a village to raise a child. My village was not pretty, they are dark dangerous and deadly. My father Rowan is an assassin. My mother was a murderer too. Both were born from murderous fathers. The other people in the village that raised me are just as bad. Callum, my uncle of sorts, is the kingpin of a criminal empire. He sells drugs, diamonds, weapons, people and death. There are others, none of them are anything other than evil. I am the heir to my father's murder mill, to Callum's empire and to this black hole heart that is filled with emptiness. My village is fucked up.

As a result, so am I. Nurture versus nature. My nature is screaming out for something else. I was nurtured to be a killing machine, the queen of a villainous empire and a ghost without a heart. I was nurtured into a beautiful monster, the Hummingbird. Now there's a fracture in my nature and I don't know what to do with it. I'm feeling things I have no right to feel.

My father sees beauty in death, I don't. I don't get the same rush, or the high. I don't need it like he does. I do it because it's all I know. I don't get overcome by a haze or a cycle. I do it because they do it, I do it because it's easy. I do it simply because I can. I don't want to know how to sell people, or drugs and guns, but I do. I do it because when Callum dies, it will be my empire to rule and I cannot fail. I do it for them, because of them and in spite of myself. My monster doesn't need to be fed like theirs, because my monster isn't real. I'm not a monster, I'm a black hole. I am worse than a monster because a monster can feel. I cannot. I want to feel. I'm nothing, an empty space void of anything other than the rules I was raised to obey. "If you love something kill it. Feelings have no place in our world, if you feel something you can be damn sure you will pay for it in pain and suffering."

"Stop squealing! It won't save you now." The boy whimpers as I press my heel harder into his chest. He's seen me, I cannot be seen because I simply don't exist, and so neither can he. His eyes stare down the barrel of the gun I hold in front of his face and a tear escapes down his handsome cheek. I'm done with him. The sweat of our recent sexcapades is still visible on his golden skin. I look one last time into his pretty boy blue eyes and pull the trigger. I prefer a knife, it's more fun, but I don't have time today. I have to get to work.

I really should just buy a vibrator, the clean-up would be so much easier.

Not that I clean my own mess, why have a dog and bark yourself? I dial Callum as I step over the body of my latest conquest and leave his ratty flat the way I came in—through the window. "Avery, again really?" He answers knowing exactly why I have called so early in the morning. "Sorry." I feign emotion and apologise when I'm not even a little sorry. "It has to stop. Avery, people are going to notice all the pretty boys going missing." I smile at his comment and his concern makes me laugh. I don't have a pattern so it will never be linked to one person. The men I choose are easily forgotten, unwanted and unloved and easy to manipulate. They just disappear and Callum seems to be the only one who cares. I can tell from his heavy breathing that my silence irritates him. "I will send someone to fix it, text me the fucking address and get yourself to fucking work, now!" he shouts at me before ending the call. It's like having two dads, only my actual dad could care less that I kill a guy every so often. My father may have taught me how to do many things but care isn't one of them. He's dead inside. He cares about nothing other than my beloved dead mother. Nothing. He's the most broken person you will find in this world. He cared once and the universe made him pay dearly for it. He won't love me, because loving her killed him. He's just a living ghost. If he loved me, he would die or chose to live, but he doesn't love me, so he exists in his limbo where nothing affects him. No one loves me.

I better go to work before Callum has a fucking aneurism.

I slide into my little red Jaguar, my painted nails match the car's colour, the deep roar of the engine is like injecting myself with pure adrenalin and I cannot wait to floor it. The speed and rebellion of driving a car my father loathes gives me a small rush. I smile as I drive away from the seedy student building and back towards the city. I shouldn't do this so close to campus and other people, I could easily get caught, but I liked the way he touched me. He was worth the added risk, usually I pick boys who won't be easily missed. Loners and out of town students, those that fly under the radar or friends and families. There is nothing like sex, murder and a fast car to start the week off right.

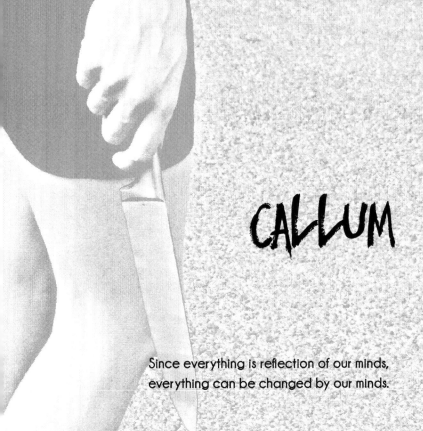

CALLUM

*Since everything is reflection of our minds,
everything can be changed by our minds.*

AFTER SHANNON'S DEATH, things were out of control. I felt a deep loss yet I was glad she was gone. I can't forgive her for what she did. I also can't forgive myself for making her do it. I know in my gut that my actions fuelled hers. She gave me a death sentence. Even though I loved her, she will still manage to kill me.

I have an inability to control the devil that beats within my heart. It felt as if the cement block dragging me to the bottom of the ocean had been cut lose, but I was still drowning. The police questioned me relentlessly for days about the poison they found in the room, why we had returned and where had I been? They pushed all my buttons over and over again until I was at the point where I was either going to murder someone or simply leave again. All of a sudden, the Police Captain came to see me after hours. I was a mess, hungover and trembling from the reality that not only did the woman I loved die, she had killed me too. I had spent days drowning myself in the bottles of whiskey that saved me from actually having to feel the truth. She killed me, she fucking killed me.

"Mr O'Reilly, we have spoken with your sister Amya. I'm terribly sorry not only for your loss, but for what you wife has done to you. I apologise for the pain our investigation has caused, I'm closing the case as a suicide but let me say this

Mr O'Reilly, I will however be watching you. I know who you are." His tone did nothing to hide the veiled threat. He would be a problem for me and I knew it. Amya spoke with them, I thought she'd left. She had, but she took the time to tell them about Shannon, my sister still cared about me.

"Thank you, Captain Swanepoel, but you haven't a clue who I am. I would like time to grieve my wife in peace now."

He stood and shook my hand before he left me with one last question.

"You wouldn't happen to know a Mr. Renzo Baldini, now would you?" I smiled at his audacity and just how close he was skating to the truth, but shook my head.

"No Captain, should I?"

"Oh, I think you already do. Goodbye, Callum." He walked out of my home and stepped closer to his own end. I couldn't have the likes of him digging around in my life. I needed to get my shit in order and start living again, yet I felt lost and without purpose. Shannon had consumed my mind and heart for so long and now, twenty years on, I'm still haunted by her. Rowan is just a shadow of what he was before, all that was left was the assassin, the person died with Lauri and my sister left us behind to find her peace. She spoke to the police, but I know she's gone from my life and she deserves that. Her husband, Robin and her deserve something more than the death that seems to shadow me everywhere I go. All I have left is that little girl with pigtails and devil eyes.

The afternoon I buried the wife I both loved and hated, I set the past four years to rest in the ground alone. She didn't deserve to be with the ones I loved so I put her cold body in a state cemetery with all the droves of dead bodies no one cared about. Interned between a John Doe and some young child this God forsaken country had claimed too young. My beautiful, deadly, poisonous bride was gone and I was a man broken by love and left to die from her. I knew it was true, I would die because of loving Shannon, I knew it the minute I saw her and again when I knew I loved her, yet I ignored that voice in my head that said stay away.

Now, twenty years after she started killing me, I sit alone here, the dialysis machine whirring next to me as I slowly lose my battle with the death she gave to me out of love. When I'm like this, my broken fucking humanity at the surface, I'm almost always forced into memories of my life, most of them are painful. A little boy lying with his dead mother or holding the gun that would rip his best friends' life apart. There are just a few that are what I would call good and surprisingly most of those are with Shannon. I loved her. The wrong kind of love, but it didn't hurt any less than the real love I never found in this life.

Now I sit here looking back on my life and I know I've made yet another horrible mistake—Avery. I have had a hand in creating a woman who is possibly worse than Shannon. She's so emotionally barren that I'm sure she has no heartbeat, but it had to be this way. This way she cannot be hurt like we have, now she can survive this world we have created around us. The mob is dying out and in its place, a new business is growing. One that shrouds the rot of crime we've perpetuated for years. I sit at the head of my empire like I always dreamed of and now I wish I had different dreams. Instead of shipping bodies away to their deaths, I wish I had one to lie with me at night. In the place of the drugs we make and sell, I wish I had a cure for my disease and rather than being king of all of this, I would go back to being the prince just to have felt real love, even for a second. I made all the wrong choices and now I lie with them in my bed instead of someone to hold me as I die.

The loud ringing of my phone drags me back to the present, her name is on the screen which means only one thing this early on a Monday morning and I don't even have to answer it to know what's happening. Avery has been having fun and now I have to clean up her broken toys again. I'm tired, so very fucking tired of this life and as I watch this stupid machine that stops me from dying. I wish it wouldn't because I'm ready to give up. I'm ready to stop going to the ends of the earth just to stay alive, this is the last time I am going to sit here and do this.

I have a few final things to get in place before I can die though. I have to bring my insurance policy and little brother home to help the devil queen run my business, ensuring we have a future and I need to lay some demons to rest.

I hang up on the headache that is Avery and ring her father, it's about time he started to deal with this shit, I'm not going to be here forever. She has spiralled out of control since I refused her offer of a kidney to save my life. She just cannot accept that I no longer want to live, she has an attachment to me and I need to break it before she gets hurt more. I'm exactly where I said I never wanted to be. When Renzo begged me to die, I said I would fight to live. I'm finished fighting.

I understand his need to give up and die. The will to suffer longer has left me. We can only lose what we cling to and it's time Avery starts letting go so that her suffering can be less than mine.

EIRAN

When there is no enemy within the enemies outside cannot hurt you.

I WAIT FOR THE CALL that I know Callum is going to make to me any moment. I've been watching her. I always watch her. So I know he will phone us to go clean up the pieces of another fuck-toy that is left in the wake of Avery Spillane-Leahy, also known as the Hummingbird. Most Mondays start this way, sometimes they don't make it all the way to Monday morning and I get a call earlier, but she liked this one. I could see it in her eyes, the way she trailed her hand down his chest as they left the nightclub where she found him. A pretty boy with a tan and surfer hair, his icy blue eyes the opposite of me in every way. They're always the opposite of me, but they are never the same. Being a clever killer dictates that she has to be careful to make sure they're all different. Surfer boy made her happy for a bit, she smiled her dazzling smile and her eyes lit up when he made her laugh. His pretty clean skin and wholesome fresh look are almost too perfect, the way he has that charming boyish smile that melts girls panties right off. He is so normal, the one thing she craves to make her happy, a little slice of normal. Avery is not happy very often, in fact, she's perpetually sad or raging angry.

I watched her slip out the window and down the fire escape stairs a few minutes ago, her hair was messy and she looked like the morning after. Even like that she is beautiful, she has always been a thing of beauty that I cannot look away from. She hates me, she would kill me if she could. You see, I stole something from her and I can't give it back, so she will never forgive me. So now I work for them, forever paying back the mistakes I made. I was just a young gangster on the street trying to make my boss notice me, she was just another job to me and it all turned horribly wrong. Now she is an obsession, and infection I can't cure.

My phone vibrates in my pocket as she speeds away in that fucking conspicuous red car.

"This is Eiran." I answer it as if I wasn't expecting the call. I am always expecting it.

"I'm sending you an address, clean it up and make it go away." Callum's voice carries into my ears, he's my boss. No, Avery is my boss and he is our boss. "Eiran, do it right please." He hangs up, please is about as courteous as he gets. The message with the address is a wasted effort. He doesn't know I'm already here. I use the time to phone my team and get them here. A bunch of street criminals with a special skill for cleaning up the scene of the crime and making it seem as if it never happened. I have been cleaning her mess for nine years now, and I have to say she doesn't have her father's finesse for a clean kill. No, Avery likes to make them bleed.

The second floor flat is a typical guy pad, stand up paddle boards line the entrance—I knew he was a surfer. The place smells of cheap weed and sex. Oh Callum is going to go postal if she's still high when she gets to work. Her lover's clothes are on the floor in front of the beat up brown couch and I pick them up to bag them. The glass hubbly and weed lie on the battered coffee table, I point at them so that Frankie can clean them into a wet bin. We scour the area making sure there's no sign of her or his corpse being here. I make my way through the living room to the door that must lead to his room and his dead body. The messy clutter of meaningless crap that fills the space is almost suffocating, there's no order to any of it. What's worse, the clutter is covered in a layer of dust that could suffocate you if disturbed. As I step through the door into his room, I note the faded navy blue bedding is tossed in a pile next to the bed with him on top of it; they look like his mother picked them out for him. At least she did us the courtesy of using a gun and not her favourite knife, there's only a blood pool beneath him and most of it is caught in the bedding which we will bag and remove.

Within minutes, the naked body of her dead play thing is wrapped in plastic and put into a municipal dustbins that we wheeled in with us so we can exit the building without raising too much suspicion. Being dressed in uniforms and driving a cleaning service vehicle, we go unnoticed for the most part. His body will be dumped in the acid reservoir at a local chemical manufacturing plant where he will dissolve and disappear for good.

After he's dissolved into chemical soup and the job completed, I stop at home to take a quick shower before I go into the office. I smell of stale dagga smoke and dust, it makes me want to gag. As I let the hot water wash away the dirt of another clean-up, my mind goes back to her, the way she moved as she exited the building, the way she slipped into her car. The way my heart beats when I watch her.

I touched her once, she was so soft in my hands, her pale soft skin was like silk. I kissed her once, she kissed me back—a kiss of death, her pink lips claiming mine. I held her for a second and the world stood still, my heart beat faster and dreamed of love for a second. Then I raped her and I believed she let me, her body melted to mine as she screamed and yelled no until she had no air left in her lungs. The feeling of her virginity tearing and taking what was not mine, the power of her body responding to me, fuelled the villain below the face of a boy. In my mind, I was loving her because her body was coming apart, shattering and shuddering with every thrust, then she took out a knife and cut me to ribbons. I had a moment of weakness, a delusional second where I believed she loved me so I cut her free. In that moment she disarmed me, I didn't even know it was happening. I stole from her and now I pay for it every fucking day. You see she didn't kill me, no she would rather make me suffer. I had a moment of weakness where I touched heaven and it lead me to a lifetime in hell. Being a gangster on the streets, peddling drugs and kidnapping rich girls like her for money was easy, I was just a cog in the machine. When Avery paid her own ransom in exchange for my half dead bleeding body. I wanted to die, because I knew she was going to kill me every single day. Slipping on my jeans and a white shirt, I shake off the feelings and get ready to be cold, empty and impervious to her. That is the only way to survive. Survive is about all you can hope for when it comes to Avery.

AVERY

You will not be punished for your anger,
you will be punished by your anger.

BEING IN THE OFFICE all day is the worst kind of torture, I hate the way the four walls box me into the role of business woman. The corporate clothes I wear to hide me from the stuck up people that I need to interact with. You see, in here it is the civilised criminals I deal with. When I wield a gun or a knife, it is the other kind of monster that I'm working with. Neither are good, but it's this organised evil that I hate the most. I tap my heel under the desk as I comb over the details of a diamond deal that needs to be closed before the end of the week. I have some very beautiful raw stones coming in from the Lesotho highlands and they need to be cut and polished and ready to sell fast.

I hate diamonds, they are not this girl's best friend, besides girls like me don't need friends. The filthy stones that come from the despair and death of so many are not the jewels I want to adorn my body. I prefer the pure beauty of art. As long as I can remember I wanted to have the same beautiful drawings as my parents had adorn my body. My mother's was a work of art. My father still turns heads with his coloured skin, the only space left on him are his lower legs and his face. Yet my exposed skin is still clean and pure, but beneath my clothes, a tapestry of colour is being woven. I'm painted in secrets and lies. There's a line dividing me into two halves, from my chest to my crotch. One half is a colourful picture of birds and flowers, skulls and blood. There are numbers hidden in the pictures. Ugly numbers. Dad taught me that treasures are something far rarer than diamonds, something clean and completely out of reach for those who live in our world. Things like innocence, trust, hope and worst of all love are the gems that will never adorn the crown of this princess. Instead I have, blood, bones, diamonds and sorrow as the stones that shine in my tiara. I'm going to be in charge of all of this forever and I accepted that a long time ago.

I hear the heavy footfalls of Eiran's boots as he stomps down the hall towards his office which is at the end of the passage. Our offices are close enough that I can watch him and he can watch me, but far enough away that I'm out of his reach. He thinks I don't know that he is my shadow, a silent presence that reminds me of my weakness and humanity when all I want is to forget. I need to embrace this life because Callum is dying fast and then it will be all that I have left. I know he cleaned up another dead lover this morning and that thought brings a smile to my face. They all get what he wants and cannot have. I love the slow torture of taunting him. A part of me belongs to Eiran you see, he took it from me and now he's paying for it. Nothing's free in this life and my virginity cost Eiran his soul.

Slam.

His door shuts behind him. I have a weakness—him. My mind doesn't focus when I'm near him, my body betrays me wanting feelings that I know I'm not permitted to have. My eyes get lost on his looks, my heart pounds with the same fear that it did as he raped me. I know he wears scars of my knife all over him, I cut him to ribbons. Denying the truth is futile, I didn't care that he raped me. His touch was a spark that set my demons alight and I have never again found the same relief. I should have killed Eiran like all the others since then, but as I filleted his flesh from the bones and his blood dripped on the floor by my bare feet a better idea struck me. I decided to keep him, a trophy for anyone who decided to try and take what wasn't theirs. As the blood of my virginity dried on my thighs and I burned from his assault, I learned a very valuable lesson about myself. I want to feel I crave the rush it brings me, but I loathe feelings. Emotions let me give up the fight that roars in me so that Eiran could make my body feel, but I will never let my heart feel again. I will feel with my body only. Touch me, I need to feel it, but don't come near my heart or you'll disappear.

My phone causes the desk to vibrate and snaps me out of my stupid moment of nostalgic lust. Grabbing it as I rise from my seat, I shove my chair back and I get ready to go and sell some diamonds and souls to a devil in pretty boy clothes.

Swinging my keys back and forth between my fingers as I walk to the lift, the jingle of the small metal key chain soothes me and I'm smiling again as the doors open. If I could whistle, I'd be whistling a happy song, there is nothing quite like being a murderer in the morning. Callum is on the other side, his sick body wasting away right before us, his eyes are grey where they used to be vivid green. The colour of his skin is ashen and the years of heartache have been etched into every wrinkle. It's as if dying slowly has painted him black and white, the grey of living in purgatory has seeped out of his pores. I kiss his cheek as we pass each other, the sorrow evident in his eyes as he watches the doors close between us. There used to be nothing between us at all. Now, there is so much in the way that we will never get past it all. I failed him and he hurt me. Neither of us will ever admit our faults, I don't know how to say sorry because I'm not.

It's lunch time before I reach the diamond store, the secret of dirty business is make it look so clean no one looks twice. The up market dealer in the huge shopping mall is far from seedy and suspicious while attracting rich housewives, business men and collectors are their clients. Death, blood and shiny rocks are the merchandise of choice. The silly electronic chime goes off as I enter the shop, plush carpet beneath my feet and the dirt of diamonds all around me.

"Avery." Sam greets me in his overly feminine voice, I have no idea how he even gets himself into those tight pants. "Sam." I air kiss him as he takes my hand in a limp handshake and starts to lead me to the back of the shop. I'm royalty here. Their books show that I spend a fortune on jewellery. I don't. I do supply them with illegal diamonds that allow them to turn massive profits. "I missed you, beautiful, what have you got for me today?" He continues our fake conversation for the benefit of the slutty looking sales girls in the shop. I'm amazed at these men here to buy rings that promise forever and the sales woman's boobs are what gets them to blow all their money.

"I need some stones cut to move elsewhere and emeralds from Zambia are for you, Sam." I'm not in the mood for chatting. I never am. I cannot relate to these people, they're criminals but they have no idea what blood feels like between your fingers or what the smell of a smoking gun is like. No, they are still normal. Clean and untainted by the true horror of their precious stones.

"Oh, I love emeralds. The green is always so amazing and once you cut them, they come alive." He answers as if I care. Emeralds remind me of the tears in Callum's eyes after I cut Eiran to pieces and they found me. I fucking hate them, they represent disappointment and loss. There is no beauty in that.

The stones are tipped onto a small table where each one is inspected under a magnifying glass and light, he makes a detailed list of every stone. It takes forever. "So I heard Callum is getting really bad." His attempt at small talk is scratching at a raw wound. I ignore him. Not only do I not care to discuss it, we do not need the world knowing how sick the boss is. Not yet. I am not sure this web of crime is ready for a lady boss. They won't have a choice, but I know there will be upheaval. Not everyone is going to accept me and that's okay, I expect it. There will be war when Callum dies and I'm ready to fight it.

"Are we done yet, Sam? I don't have all fucking day." I snap out at him. He rolls his eyes and picks up the shop phone. "Lydia, go get Miss Leahy some lunch while we finish up choosing her next piece. Vegetarian, no meat." He gives me a shut up look and carries on sorting the small pile of gemstones. I don't eat meat, Callum taught me to be weary of food, after all, he was poisoned for years. That aside, I cannot bear the thought of eating something bloody. Fish, even chicken I can stomach but red meat makes me want to hurl.

"Meet any cute guys yet?" His idle chatter carries on.

"A few, none that you'll see around here." I know my reputation is clear in our circles even though he would never say it aloud. "You like university boys too much, Avery? You need to look for a man. One that wears an actual suit not dreadlocks and a wetsuit." The thing is, people would miss someone in a suit. A silly college boy doing stupid shit and disappear all the time. "Sam, you have far too much time to think about men. I'm not looking for nor do I need a man in my life. There isn't room for it all." The silent but underlying truth silences him for a few minutes. I am going to be consumed by this business when Callum is gone, I won't have time for fun.

"I had lunch with a hot guy from the Gucci store last week." He could date a Gucci salesman, it would be a good fit. Dirty diamond dealer and fashion dunce. "And?" I ask not really caring about his answer but keen to pass the time. The silly girl from the front brings me a healthy sandwich and a cold pressed juice from the vegan shop around the corner and dumps one next to Sam before slinking back out of the office again.

"I don't like her." I make the statement aloud when I really shouldn't have.

"Neither do I. I'm thinking of reasons to fire her, give me a chance." He answers without looking up from the shiny stones in front of him, he is drawn to them where I am repulsed by them. We see very different things in them. By the time Sam is done the entire afternoon has passed and I'm loathe to return to the office, but I always do. I end every day running through the days' work with Callum and tormenting Eiran.

I STOP AT A LOCAL jazz lounge on the way home from the office, I know Eiran has followed me. I know he's watching me I want him to watch. I get off knowing he can see me with them. I sip on a glass of wine from my family's wine farm, each vintage is now in some way named after my mother. Rowan never let her go, he's still mourning her absence every single day. I roll up my sleeves and unbutton my collar exposing my chest, allowing my true colours to leak out for the world to see. I lean back in the leather chair and listen to the humming of the music and the people. The eclectic mix of artists and business people, the rich and poor melt together over booze and melody. The smoke and wine mix to fill the air with life and lies, no one in here is who they seem. I like simple places like this, where I can let my guard down and live, even just for a little bit. My foot swings to the music and I watch the people fill up the space. The university students love the place and the crowd is young and vibrant, couples dance in between the tables and the smoke and wine smell mingles with lust. Watching them rub up against each other makes me horny and I squeeze my thighs together, but it just makes it worse. My eyes begin to wander, looking for someone that could be used for a little stress relief tonight. A wicked smile starts to form on my face as I catch a glimpse of Eiran across the street. He's sitting on a restaurant balcony, eating food he doesn't like so that he can watch me. I know he hates curry so the Indian restaurant is definitely not his idea of a good dinner. He knows I'm hunting, he knows me too well. There are two older men sitting a bit away from me, they're up against the wall trying to look without being seen. *I see you boys, let's play.*

Sam arrives catching my eye with a small wave and a shake of his head, I wish I could say we were friends but I don't have friends. If I did, Sam would be one. I usually save this sort of recreation for the weekends, today I'm antsy and something's off. Something is making me want to kill. I start flirting with my eyes, they notice me—they always do. It's too easy, they are all so predictable. When I walk by them to the bathrooms, their eyes follow me first, I notice the subtle elbow and whisper as one eggs the other on. He shakes his head as I disappear around the corner, he's a good guy, he won't follow me in here, how boring. I'll get him on the way back. Or them. I like the idea of them, anything that will scratch this itch right now. I don't need to pee, nor would I use the filthy restrooms if I did, but I stand in the stall for a few minutes, reading the graffiti and waiting a believable amount of time. I stare down at the uncomfortable heels that have become my uniform anytime I'm not in my own house. I see my face in the shiny patent finish, a face I barely recognise anymore. I hear the band taking a break outside, the lull in music and buzz in voices alerts me to the fact this bathroom will soon be full of women so I flush the toilet I didn't even sit on and exit. The long passage is filling with bodies moving against me, I hope I haven't missed the two men I hoped to prey on. A familiar feeling starts to creep up my spine, I stand a little straighter and I smile. I like this feeling. The pins and needles of doing something that is wrong. I know it's wrong. I crossed the line between what I do and who I am a long time ago. Incapable of separating killing for a job and fun, I became a murderer and not a hired hit. I like being wrong. It cancels out the need to have feelings that would fill the gaping hole in my heart. No one is meant to love a killer so my solitude is validated by what I chose to do.

The two men have moved to the bar and I see the blond one looking over his shoulder, checking the passage entrance. I sit at their table in the hope that if they won't follow me, I will just join them. I see the smile and the chatter exchanged as they notice me on their walk back, too damn easy. He runs his hand through the long mop on his head and licks his lips, I have whet his appetite and he's about to feed my demons. His friend is bit more introverted, he walks one step behind as if there is no way I would be here for him, he's used to being second best to his hot friend. Only I don't see the appeal, the shy one intrigues me. His beard and neat hair tell me he is a straight line sort of fellow. I am going to make this good looking blond friend feel like he does—insignificant and unworthy. Mind games excite me, I love to fuck with people's feelings. I almost want to laugh out loud as I watch the two of them hesitate before they finally approach the table.

"Hello gents." I greet them looking only at the one with dark hair, his eyes are down as if he is embarrassed by my attention or avoiding it at all costs. Something tells me he isn't what meets the eye and I feel a prickle of warning. Blondie offers me his drink as he sits. "No thanks, that looks better." I point at his friend's whiskey, five points for choosing a big boy drink and not a fucking beer. He seems loathe to give it to me but slides it over, his friend sits between us, I can sense he is used to the attention, probably a bit of a man slut. "So are you going to tell me your name before I drink from your glass?" Eyes on the man across from me, ignore his buddy the game is going to get fun. "Mathew," he stutters out. Gah, I just knew it would be some proper name. I bet he went a private school and has finished university with a law degree or something equally boring. I glance at his friend, waiting for him to answer me, I know he will whether I wanted to know his name or not. Killing him is going to be fun, I bet he cries like a girl. "Owen. And what's your name beautiful?" The way he drags out beautiful makes me grind my teeth. He thinks I'm some silly girl who models or cuts hair. I'm so tired of being underestimated.

"Avery." I answer looking at Mathew as I sip on his drink. "You have good taste Mathew, expensive but good." He smiles and I can see Owen's confusion in my peripheral vision, I don't care about him though. I like what I'm doing to Mathew—he's is smiling now and sitting up straighter.

"It should be, he's a doctor." Mr Jealousy pipes in from outside our little bubble and my attention snaps around to him my expression should tell him enough. *I want to murder you—run away while you can.*

"And what do you do, Owen?" I ask because I have to keep him a little engaged not because I care. I can guess before he even says it. "I'm a gynaecologist." I knew it would be something ridiculous. He bores me, make no mistake, he's something to look at, strong jaw, just enough stubble to make the girls wet their panties and arms that tell me he goes to some yuppie gym. Oh, Owen is a good looking lad, but there is no mystery. What you see is what you get—good looking half-wit that looks at vaginas all day. "What do you do, Avery?" I love this part, I slip my hand into my small bag and take out a business card, my red nails click as I set it down in front of him.

Avery Leahy.

CEO O'Reilly Holdings International.

A name that's plastered on billboards all over the globe. I've been in business magazines and spoken at the University that the two of them most likely attended. I eyeball him waiting on a response but he's dumbstruck so I go back to Mathew who has a huge smile because I managed to silence his cocky friend.

"Dance with me, Doctor Mathew." I play on his ego a little but really I just want to touch him. He looks like he feels good under those stiff clothes, I like touching. I turn my eyes downward a little so I'm not as intimidating as I usually am as he holds out a hand and stands up next to me. Too easy. I look out the windows so that I can see across the street as Eiran sits drinking and watching. His venomous eyes stare at me and I can see even from here he clenches his jaw. Mathew's hand settles into the small of my back. It feels good, I like the warmth as he guides me to a small corner where there's just enough room to dance if you get really close to each other. I glance over Matthew's shoulder to see Owen sipping his beer, I've battered his ego and he looks upset—shame poor him. Mathew smells good as he pulls me close to him, a little more in control than I thought he would be. I can feel him as he begins to sway me, leading the dance. I knew private schools make the boys learn to dance. My head rests perfectly in his neck as I'm a little shorter than he is and I see his pulse right before my eyes, I imagine his blood pouring from it. The hands that were so gentlemanly earlier creep a little lower resting almost on my ass and I suck in a breath so he knows I noticed. The deep notes of the music lull me into smooth movements with him, I like this feeling. I always like this feeling, when they don't know any better and try to seduce me. My eyes open enough to see the fury brewing in his friend, left at the table as we get sensually acquainted between all these other bodies. Mathew leans his head down a little lower so I can feel his breath—the breath I plan to rob him of later on. Just a little longer and I know the temptation of kissing me will be too much and his gentlemanly control will crumble. I pull my body flush with his. I can feel that it affects him, men cannot hide their lust like we can. I won't lie, if I was wearing knickers they'd be soaked because Mathew is good at this. He gets overlooked by the ladies often but when they notice they are rewarded. I run a hand through the hair in the nape of is neck and he growls in my ear. "You make it hard to be a gentleman, Avery." Oh, I know I do. "So don't be a gentleman then." I hiss back on his neck so that he can feel my lips and I know I've won. Mathew kisses me, some people notice others don't, Owen notices and leaves for the bar—well there goes half the fun. His tongue tastes of the whiskey I like to drink and his hands are rough as he holds me tighter on my exposed skin. Kissing is the most intimate thing in the world to me, I can tell so much about them when I kiss them. My heart beats a little faster and I feel my breath hitch as I swallow hard to hide the physical reaction I'm having. I hold on a little tighter and push harder against him seeking the connection. My body responds to touch, not emotion, the physical feel of his body against me is what elicits the response. The warmth rising up my chest, the buzz of nerve ending coming to life. Touch me, kiss me I live for that high of being touched. You cannot disguise or fake a kiss, Mathew is filled with hidden passion and secrets. I open my eyes after he stops, my breath is taken away just for a minute. I love this part where I feel it. No emotion, not the electric shock of sex dancing through me, the pulse of lust beating in my veins. He pulls me even closer and keeps dancing, I wonder if he's afraid I'll be gone if he lets go. Over his shoulder, I look across the street to the parked cars and see Eiran standing behind one, his eyes bore holes into mine and I smile at him. I take a hand off of Mathew's back and slide it between us so I can feel his hard on through his pants. He stiffens as I touch him, and grabs my hand to pull it away. He grabs my ass hard and bites my earlobe before he whispers again, "I would prefer if you saved that for when we are alone, Avery. I don't like to share and I especially don't like Owen to see when I win." He thinks he won.

"So let's go be alone, Mathew, because I like the way this feels." I slide my hand back there just for a second and he grips me by the wrist and drags me out the front door. He is hard and moves with determination and no consideration for me, I like this. The pavement is uneven and I'm stretched to keep up with him as he strides. His grip is so tight it's biting into my skin. I see Eiran. He wants to take a step closer. He hates this as much as I love it—his hesitation makes my heart flutter—he wants to stop me, but he can't. Mathew stops and opens the door of a large SUV and he helps me in before kissing my cheek. I have a fleeting minute where I think I might just be the prey this time; gentleman Mathew has a vicious side and I see that twinkle of darkness in his eyes. I have to cross my legs to try and control the pull he has on my lady parts. I recognise a villain when I see one, and the slightly shy guy from inside was a disguise for the benefit of others.

I like the silent type, I usually keep them around a little longer than the others and Mathew isn't a college boy, he's a man. An older man that I plan to enjoy. When we stop at a block of upmarket waterfront apartments just a short way from the bar he turns and speaks for the first time. "I will take you to fetch your car when we are done." When we are done? What the fuck does he think he gets to decide when I am done? "And when will that be?" I ask with a raised eyebrow. He doesn't answer me. He just gets out and who comes to open my door, I'm not sure—gentleman or predator? It doesn't matter because the only part of me that has any sway right now is between my thighs.

The garden apartment on the ground floor is very modern but lived in, I look around taking it in. Nice and easy to clean such smooth surfaces, Eiran will be happy, carpets are always such a bitch. A spaniel barks at me through the glass doors and I smile, I like pets but my dad never allowed me to have one. I think he was worried I would kill it if he did. I got Eiran instead. I'm handed a glass of good whiskey that I don't plan to drink, I'm far too aware of how easy it would be for a doctor to drug me, I'm a criminal, not a fool. I set the glass and my bag down in a spot where I can get to easily if I need them. Mathew closes the blinds, shutting the dog and the world out before he returns to me, lifting my chin up he kisses me again. This time no one is watching and he has no need to be civil. He bites my lip and I like it too much, I groan in appreciation. Pulling his shirt from his trousers so I can feel his skin, I feel something else I missed earlier—a gun. What sort of a doctor needs a gun? I remind myself of where we live and that everyone actually needs a gun. I push that little alarm that goes off inside my head aside because his hands grabbing my ass and pulling my hair feels so good. Standing between the living room and his kitchen, I let myself feel. Not emotions but the physical touch of him against me. The push and pull of control dragging us back and forth with each touch, bite and kiss. God he was making me forget who I am, he dominated me like no other had ever tried. He was not afraid of a woman with power. I'm usually numb to the charms of men, I choose them young and naive on purpose. This is breaking rules and moving too far from my comfortable predictable patternless pattern. Oh fuck me this feels like heaven. He's stripping me bare of the control I always have and I like it too much to stop him. "Let's go, little lady." He growls pulling himself from me and walking down a small hallway that leads to the lion's den. I normally give the orders, I don't know why I just follow him. I'm having a brain malfunction and I really should get out of here but my stupid cunt is begging for him to fuck me and I know that's exactly what he is going to do when we get to the bedroom. He kicks off his shoes at the door of the master bedroom and while looking at me, unholsters his gun and lays it down on the dresser. Even from where I stand, I can see the safety is off and it's loaded. His holster falls on the floor where he stands. The doctor is not what he seems. I ignore it because I have a knife in my stockings that I know he has felt already so he knows that I am more than meets the eye. The voices in my head are screaming loudly as he unbuttons his dress shirt and loses his cufflinks. Motherfuck, how can I listen to them when that is in front of me. His friend was not hot, that is hot. That is man, not boy, or young man—man, defined and perfect each muscle sculpted not from gym, but from being active. I'm standing dead still, rooted to the spot as a watch the gentleman transform into something quite different as he disrobes, his smile isn't seductive—it's predatory. My plan to hunt has backfired. I will still kill him, maybe not tonight but eventually he will have to go. His pants are loosened and hang on his hips, his chest is on display for me, there's a slight dusting of hair. Not enough to be gross but not bare like the boys I usually undress. I look past him to the photograph hanging above his bed, a silhouette of a man on the shore with a surf board above his head—he likes the water. The room is clinically neat and nothing else in it has any personality at all. I didn't notice him stalking closer to me while I was distracted with taking him it all in, until his smell filled my nostrils. "You have far too many clothes on, and I don't allow shoes on the hardwood floors." I robotically respond to him by sliding out of my heels and unbuttoning my shirt. I'm waiting for the moment he sees what I hide below the surface. His eyes widen and I see the bad guy in them smiling, his tongue licks his bottom lip and I know I don't stand a chance of surviving this unchanged. "You are quite the work of art, Avery. I always wondered what you would be hiding under the stiff work clothes." Fuck he knows me, or of me. I should never ignore the voices. I stiffen at his comment, "Oh, I know who you are, I almost couldn't believe it when I saw that business card. I never had the pleasure of meeting any of the other bosses before."

He's one of *our* doctors, that's a good and a bad thing. I have nothing to live or die for so I just leave the thoughts behind and for a minute or two I chose to let this happen. "You work for me don't you, Mathew. I bet your name's not Mathew."

"I work for Callum and in here, I don't work for anyone. In here—" He points around the room. "There is only one boss and it's me, Avery. Leave that knife next to my gun then get naked on my bed." His boldness both infuriates and entices me. I slide my skirt down my legs and before I can step out of it, he removes the pretty garter that holds my weapon. My knife is now in his hands. He's in my personal space, looking into my eyes and I know he sees me. He traces the line down my middle with the blade of my defence all the way from my breast bone to my belly, he stops just before he gets to the part of me that drips for him. Lust is a demon that can leave us all defenceless to our needs. "This is a surprise I must say." He drags the blade slightly lower to where the artwork licks my cunt. "Did it hurt?" he continues as I nod truthfully, because it hurt like a bitch when I had it done. That grin that says so much is back and he presses the blade a little harder against my skin before he lets out a soft rumble and says, "Not nearly as much as I'm going to hurt it." His violent words make my insides tense in anticipation. This is the shit you read about in dirty books. This cannot be real. He holds the blade to my throat as he turns me around, reminding me just how very real this is. I'm not in control. I find that thought strangely comforting and freeing. Why should I always have it all together? I want to fall apart, and I want to fall apart with this man, whoever he is. "What's your real name?" I ask because I have this intimate need to know the real person not the front that I met in the bar. He's a doctor, that's the only truth he's told so far.

"Mathew."

"Don't lie."

"I'm not. Mathew is my name."

"It is not."

"Avery is your name, you don't even lie about it, why would I?"

"I can just tell it isn't who you are." My sixth sense tingles with a bullshit warning.

"Mathew is my second name. So it's no lie and I'm not sharing who I am with you, Avery. This isn't about *you*. This is about the desire dripping between your thighs and a need that I have to shove my cock in you and possess you, so shut the fuck up and just let go." I hadn't even realised my death grip on his knife wielding hand. I relax my fingers and drop my arm. "Good girl, go lay down." *Good girl? Something I was never told, something so simple but so crushing all at once. I was never anyone's good girl before.*

I let it all go, for once I don't hang onto myself at all. He hurt me, just as he promised he would. His hands smacked me, then brought me to the edge of ecstasy. His teeth tore into my flesh but his mouth made me come until my body felt broken. He hurt me and I loved it, he fucked me until I had tears and it was earth shattering. I lost myself in his torment and found pleasure I never knew existed.

Surrender is so foreign to me. I cannot get my mind to reconcile that I surrendered to him, my body adored it as I came over and over again with his vicious touch. Spent, fucked, and feeling—a place I hate to be. True to his word, he took me back, dropped me at my car and left me there. I sat in my car for a few minutes trying to reconcile what had happened when a loud knock on the window made me grab for my knife. It wasn't needed as Eiran's black eyes met mine with pure hate. I lowered the window which I normally wouldn't do for him, but tonight I am not myself.

"I don't have to clean up?" He seems bitter.

"I liked this one." I spit back and start to put the window up.

"You are playing with fire and the devil, Avery. Neither of us should be fucked with." His threat is evident, he doesn't like it when I keep them around for any amount of time. He likes it that I kill them because then I'm still his in some stupid childish way. Part of me will always be his, but no part of me wants to be.

"Fuck off, Eiran." I close the window and start my car. I wonder if he knows the doctor?

I need a stiff drink and my bed before the day starts, I hate this feeling that's bubbling up from within me and I need to numb it out quickly. Callum will notice it in a second and heaven forbid him or my father see me crumbling. No matter what I do I cannot rid my heart of the thump it makes when Eiran is involved. On the drive home, I realise something in the cavity of my soul. I felt that same fucking dreaded gut churning thump with him, it makes we want to go and kill his dog.

EIRAN

No one saves us but ourselves. No one can and no one may.
We ourselves must walk the path.

I WATCH. I ALWAYS WATCH. I want to take, touch and to fuck, but my fear stops me. The memory of the blade slicing the flesh from my bones makes me to scared to do anything more than watch her. I know that someday watching won't be enough and my willpower will defeat my fear and I will fuck her till she bleeds, but until then I keep watching. I swallow the hurt every time, each new lover is the same pain of the knife she cut me with. It's not special anymore. I unconsciously trace my scars when I think about it, I'm watching her dance with Callum's doctor now. I know that will go over like a charm when he finds out. No one will ever be right for her in their eyes, she isn't allowed to get close to people she is to be a ghost, a public face of the company and a poster child of career criminals. Her hair covers her face as it rests on his shoulder, I'm sure he can feel her breath on his skin as his hands skirt dangerously close to her ass. I can almost feel what it must be like to touch her that way, with tenderness and feral intent. I make no attempt to hide myself tonight, sometimes I do hide just so she feels secure. I know she taunts me on purpose, as if she knows I'm there watching for her. She makes it a theatrical performance. Tonight something is different, he isn't a young college guy that she can use her looks and power to push over. This is a man, a powerful man with connections and an appetite for women. I have had the pleasure of helping him out a few times, my cleaning services are not exclusive to Avery and her messy love life, it's more of a company-wide situation. I *need* to go closer. I pay for my drink and go downstairs. The air is still hot even outside and I light a smoke and stand across the street so she can see me watching her. There's something different in Avery's demon eyes tonight. I have seen it before though. That's a dangerous twinkle in the blackness of her soul, she feels something and when she feels someone pays for it, I'm still paying for those few minutes I made her heart beat. That look cost me my fucking soul, the doctor can only hope she kills him quickly.

She's falling apart. I have watched the last three months as she has gone from fine-tuned killing machine and ruthless business woman to risk taking basket case. Every day, we get closer to Callum's inevitable death and she gets a little closer to losing herself completely. My sweet Avery is scared. She's going to shit herself when she realises he's bringing in reinforcements. She doesn't share her toys well at all. His brother is going to get right under her skin, I can almost see the nuclear meltdown already. I don't bother to follow them home after I witness the fierce kiss they shared. I don't think I can manage more stab wounds tonight. They left her car here so they will have to return for it, or I will get a message to collect it anyway. My curiosity is piqued. I wonder how she'll handle a man who knows exactly who she is. A man who will take what he wants from her and not care a shit to leave her afterwards. I wish I had the power to leave Avery. I slip into the bar she just left and get a table in the corner so I can see her car where it is parked outside. The doctor's friend from earlier is chatting up two girls at the bar behind me and I'm surprised at Avery's choice tonight, he would have been the easy target a quick kill and all the satisfaction she needed. Why on earth did she choose the older man, the dangerous man and not the easy one she always picks. I send Callum a text. It's the other part of my job to tell him when she does stupid shit.

She went home with your Doc. Not the lady one either.

He doesn't respond which tells me he is feeling too sick to care what she does tonight. I just hope he isn't pissed when she kills his oncologist, corrupted doctors for the criminally wealthy are not always easy to find. Callum has an aversion to doctors in general, I heard his wife was a doctor and that she gave him cancer on purpose, but it could just be rumours, I wouldn't dare ask him. Almost ten years ago I met him. For the first time I was almost dead, the meat had been sliced off my bones and she asked to keep me. Like a pet. They saved my life, but not my soul. She took me from the rot of street gangs to the organised evil of their lives and made a place for me in her world but not in her life. She never breathed a word to anyone that I raped her. It was ours, something only we shared. It tethered us together and proved that even if she never said to me again, she loved me. I had made Avery feel something and her father and Callum were not happy about me being kept, neither of them had the balls to tell her no; so I lived. Those two men are ruled by one dictator and she knows it. Losing Callum is killing her too. She offered her own kidney to save him and the stubborn old man refused it. The point is, he's an old man and I believe he's tired of it all. He's particularly tired of Avery and all the shit she stirs up around her. I don't blame him, I grew tired of her games a long time ago.

I'm three sheets to the wind drunk by the time he brings her back for her car, I knew he wouldn't let her stay the night. He seems to be completely devoid of any attachments I think that's why Callum tolerates him. He's a fuck and run kind of guy. She looks like a child that has been sent to time out and it makes me smile, Avery didn't kill him, she didn't win this time. The vodka has made me brave and I knock on her window, making her reach for her knife before she even sees me.

"I don't have to clean up?" I'm almost sorry about it. I don't like the fact that I know they just fucked like animals I have no doubt he was rough with her. I want to be rough with her, and tender too.

"I liked this one." She snaps at me and it's a knife blade straight through my heart, even the others that she kept alive for more than one night never got a *like* form her they were simply good in bed or hard to kill. I breathe in rage and it consumes me.

"You are playing with fire and the devil, Avery. Neither of us should be fucked with." The booze that soaks my brain leaks from my mouth and I say it before I can think. She shuts the window and drives away; something has changed in her tonight. I can see it, because I see her. That fucker made her feel and I'm jealous and the green rage begins to pump through my veins with each heartbeat. It begins to eat at the fragile sanity that I cling to, I made her feel first, *she is mine. I claimed her.* I fucked her until the tears flowed down her cheeks then she skinned me alive for the way I made her heart sing. "If you even think you might love something, kill it." She told me over and over as we lay together that her anger was not over the virginity she lost or the fact I had raped her. No, she hated that I had made her aware of the emotions that I know she still hides behind the cold facade the world sees. And now that fucker made her feel it too. I dig my finger nails into my scalp because I have no hair to pull at, it doesn't grow on scars and patchy hair isn't very attractive. I want to go to her home and remind her that feelings are only for me, but I'm afraid I wouldn't live another day, but the vodka is numbing my fear and I start my car and drive. A fearless man is one you should be afraid of. Dying seems like the only answer to this pain.

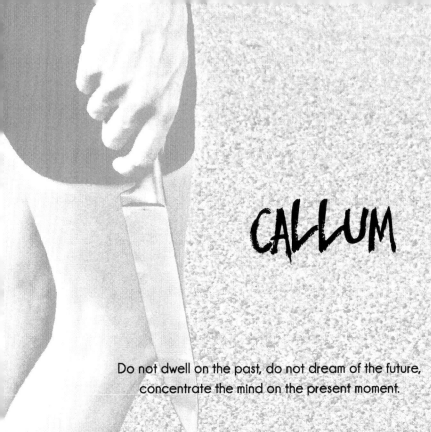

CALLUM

Do not dwell on the past, do not dream of the future,
concentrate the mind on the present moment.

I'M HAVING A DRINK with my brother, I haven't seen him since he was a boy and I sent him away to boarding school. I have two breathing blood relatives left in this world and he's one of them. Unlike Amya, he *is* in the family business. I paid a shit ton of money for him to become a lawyer and he has proved to be loyal, he has demons as do we all but his seem to be under control and far less noticeable than the rest of ours. Calculating is a word I would use to describe the boy that has become a man. He lived in my house, the ghost house I shared with Shannon and the place that housed my worst nightmares. He kept my affairs at home in order and now I have brought him here to keep Avery from letting everything fall apart with her. Harmon is exceptionally clever, but he isn't smart. He is socially inept and doesn't play well with humans. He's more of a solitary savage. He likes silly women who he can manipulate without having to waste too much energy or time on.

"I don't understand why I'm here, Callum? Honestly I have no clue why I'm even alive. You killed everyone else." Harmon is bitter about having to come here, I made him come alone and his little paralegal girlfriend had to stay behind. I would say he is broken hearted but I fear he has no heart like the rest of the family. "Somethings are best left unexplained, Harmon, I need you here because I'm

going to die. It will be sooner not later and my plan for the future has failed me."
Well not entirely she was never my whole plan, just a part of a bigger one.

"You mean the infamous Avery Leahy has let you down, your criminal prodigy
has fallen apart." The cackle tells me he thinks she's a failure. She isn't, she's just
lost right now. He's determined to anger me it would seem. As I feel the madness
that resides in me take over my mind. I'm reminded that I no longer have the
strength to go crazy. I have to let the insanity live inside me with no way out.

"Would you rather be dead? Because I can tell you that unless you adjust your
fucking attitude, I will kill you before she gets a chance and believe me, she's going
to try." I threaten him again and he seems to calm down enough for us to talk
about what it is I need from him. The legal team have done their part to ensure
that things are securely in place in the event I die quicker than I want to. I get a
message alert on my phone from Eiran, I know he's following her so it's either a
body or she is in a whiskey coma somewhere. It's nothing he cannot deal with. He
is after all, her goddamned shadow. I don't pretend to understand what they mean
to each other, but Avery brought him to the brink of death and then decided she
wanted him. He watches her every move but keeps his distance and she genuinely
seems to loathe his existence, she will kill him when she is ready. My child is a
natural born killer, it's in her blood and her heart I only wish she could be set free
because even I know that somewhere in there, is a little girl that never got to live
her life. That fact is my fault, I stole her whole life to ensure my future and I'm
not sorry I did.

I ignore the message and look at Harmon, he looks like a younger me. His
beard and slick hair are just as mine were after Shannon arrived in my life, he's a
ladies man with impeccable style. The trademark suit that I wear everyday seems to
be his disguise of choice, making him seem harmless and attractive to those who
don't now who we are. A wolf in sheep clothing.

"Harmon, you two are both the last of a legacy. There are no more after you
two, that's it. The end of the great mob families. You and her—so suck it up and
learn what I need to teach you before I can't." He sighs and stretches his body
out in the chair, the two of them are like a petrol bomb and a match, the explosion is going to come. I watch him swallow his whiskey slowly, enjoying the burn
down his throat. I allowed them to meet once when Avery visited Glasnevin with
Rowan, they didn't hit it off. I know that my death will be hard on her, Harmon
doesn't seem too bothered by the fact that I'm going to die. There's something
missing in him, empathy, he seems totally devoid of it. I may be a killer, a criminal

and a bad person but I still feel the hurt of a selected few others, I am selectively empathetic. I wonder if that's a thing? I shake off my inner thoughts and look him in the eye. "I need you, I have not asked much of you in this life, in fact, I think I have been more than giving with you, Harmon. I need you to take over from me and carry this empire forward to the next generation. You have to ensure there is a next generation."

"You made me leave my girlfriend behind, asshole. How exactly should I start procreating without a woman?" The idiot doesn't understand me.

"Not with that whore, fool. With Avery." His jaw goes slack and I'm sure I can see steam coming out of his ears as he slowly turns a deep red. "We need a power child, three families combined into one legacy."

"Are you crazy old man? Has the cancer gone into your brain? We are practically related! Her mother was your cousin."

"Yes, but not yours, we don't share the same mother, Harmon. Only our father's filthy bloodline is keeping us related. So it's a non-issue." I can see him thinking it over carefully, they are not related in any way. This little idea came to me years ago and it solves a few problems. Avery might be less volatile if she finds a partner that can be her equal and I'm ensured a blood heir to carry on the family line. If I have to fucking inject her with his sperm, I will. I need this to happen, I may have lost my mind, but this is what I want before I die. A fucking legacy and they will give it to me. I wanted a child of my own but Shannon made sure that would never happen and then I decided I would make Avery mine. The thing is, Avery belongs to no one. She's a free spirit and as much as I raised her to be my heir she doesn't want it. She's unstable and the desire needed to fuel a mob boss is missing in her. So now they can make me a real heir. My mother's blood and my father's blood in one child two families joined again only this time no one will die. Add to that the dying embers of the Leahy legacy and the child will be an untouchable in the criminal empires a ruler with blood filthier than even the most pure bred monarchs.

"Callum? Do you honestly think that the devil, bitch, murderous whore will even consider a relationship with me one and two she will be the world's worst mother and that's only if she doesn't eat her own young." I don't actually care how it is done.

"Harmon, make it fucking work. I've drawn up a contract for you." I slide the envelope across the table to him. "Half of everything is yours if you and Avery have a child together. Should that not happen you won't get any of it I will give it to

Amya, wherever the fuck she's hiding."

"You are serious?" He scrunches his brow and frowns at me waiting for me to say no, but I am deathly serious. "Have you had your head checked Callum, for real? This is crazy."

I don't appreciate being called crazy, it is my crazy that got me where I am today. I changed the mob from a bunch of thugs to a well-oiled industrial machine that rules the whole damn world. Little shit, he knows nothing about crazy. My eye catches Eiran's message still on my screen and I have a moment of pure panic, she cannot kill him. I need him to kill me when the time is right, I chose him because he does assisted suicide. Fuck it all to hell today has just been shit from start to end. I growl loudly as I dial his number still glaring at my brother.

"Eiran. She can't fucking kill him. I need him." I bark before he can even say hello.

"She didn't kill him, Callum, she likes him. God knows why but I think he may even have hurt the feelings she doesn't have," he slurs back at me.

"Are you drunk?"

"Very. I'm off the clock so it really shouldn't matter. The good doctor fucked her and dumped her back at her car. Your little nightmare is wounded."

"Eiran go home and sleep that off, I want to see you tomorrow. You need to meet my brother." I hang up on him and look up to find Harmon grinning from ear to ear shaking his head.

"Your plan is a shit one, brother. I will try but when it blows up and she kills me and you remember this conversation where I warned you." The look on his face tells me he is considering it and that's all I need right now.

"You will understand it eventually. Just don't let her fucking kill you."

I'm tired, so very tired of all of this and I want to go to bed. I get up and leave him with the contracts and a bottle of good whiskey.

"Goodnight, Harm, welcome home."

"Callum, don't tell her about this. For once just trust me, I think I understand it, but Avery most certainly won't." He is a smart man I nod and walk out the door.

"I was never going to tell her." She doesn't need to know what I have stolen from her.

EIRAN

There are only two mistakes one can make along the road to truth;
not going all the way and not starting.

'GO HOME, EIRAN.' I wish I could go home Callum, but I can't. I'm going to her and I'm going to make her feel it. I need her to know what she does to me, how these years have tortured me. She needs to understand that he can't make her feel like I did. I want her to remember those few fleeting moments where we connected. I need her to want me like I want her. I'm going to take back what has always been mine whether she wants to give it me or not. I'm breathing in and out nothing but the green rage of my jealousy and I know that I'm walking into my own murder but fuck me, I'm ready to die for her.

I sit outside long enough for her to start drinking, you see the sting of the hot doctor's rejection will drive her straight to the bottle. Wine, it won't be, whiskey she will drink her mother's wine, straight out of the bottle her plump lips wrapping around it is as she drowns out the tickle of feelings that has reared its ugly head tonight. I'm patient because I know that she needs to be a little off her game if I am even to get near her. I want that lithe body beneath mine, I need her to feel me physically, emotionally and painfully I need to hurt her. If I can make her feel my pain maybe it will stop, just for a little the ache in me will dull and I can let it go.

How dare she let another in! All these years, not once have I seen her show an ounce of emotion other than the pure venomous rage when Callum said he wouldn't take her kidney. Nothing, just the dead eyes of a monster and now she chooses him to make her feel. The angel of death doctor that is just as fucking murderous as she is.

The clock is moving so slowly, I can almost feel the drag of every minute stretching out for ten. I wait, my mood just gets darker as I do nothing but remember the feel of her skin against mine. I watch, the only light is coming from the dining room and I'm sure she has passed out right there, her balcony doors wide open letting the hot night air in and making this so easy for me. I close my car door quietly and use the fire escape stairs to start my upward journey to her. When I reach her floor, I slip into the building and try her front door first. My stupid wounded angel left it unlocked allowing me to slither in. She's shrouded by the dull light from the next room where she sits on the couch staring out at the ocean. I hear something that only deepens my rage, a sniff. Her tears are mine, only mine. She cried that day as I forced myself inside her, silent tears poured down her cheeks as she shook her head, those demon eyes begging me to make her feel the love. Her eyes cried but her soft body responded to me as I made her feel the power of her orgasm over and over. The sweet precious blood of her virginity coating my dick as I shoved it past her innocence, but she wasn't innocent. No, she was already a stone cold killer. I just made her feel, I showed her something no one else ever had I made her heart beat and she responded to me. I am the only lover to have survived Avery. *Now he has spoiled that.* Later I untied her, convinced she loved me and as she straddled me and kissed me with a fiery passion. I felt the fullness of love in my heart. She whispered in my ear softly that I made her feel something so special and my cock grew hard for her again. Right before she let it slip inside her she stabbed me the first time and she continued to cut me to shreds as she fucked me until she no longer felt and all I felt was agony and the silent pull of death dragging me away.

Now she sits here, in the almost darkness, spilling her tears for another and I can't bear it, my fear no longer rules my actions, my desire to have those feelings belong to only me is far more.

"Why are you here, Eiran?" she asks without looking in my direction, she's still connected to me. I knew it.

"I came for you. I can't watch anymore." I tell her the truth, she's going to kill me no matter what happens here I have crossed an invisible line between us and that means I am a dead man.

"Why now?"

"Because he was different."

"You are right, he was."

"Why? Avery why?"

"He reminded me of you. He took what he wanted and left me with nothing but feelings." Her words are daggers of devastating truth. I'm standing right behind her now and wrap my hand around her delicate neck, she doesn't move or resist my touch. Her eyes close and her mouth opens as I lean down to where I can smell her and the wine she drowned those emotions in. "No one is like me, Avery. I'm going to take something from you again tonight."

"You can't rape me again, Eiran. You cannot take my virginity twice, I don't have anything worth taking, you asshole." She stutters out and I feel her tense under the grip of my hand.

"Oh what I'm taking from you tonight is worse than rape. I'm going to steal your emotional virginity and make you fucking feel everything you never wanted to feel." I feel her shiver not sure if it is fear or desire I continue to squeeze. "Most of all, Avery, I want you to hurt I want you to feel the agony as I fuck your heart and soul. I want to hear the sound of your broken heart shattering underneath me."

"You know I will kill you this time, Eiran?" she speaks softly her body betrays her mind and a thick lust coats her throat making her words sound like sex.

"Oh I'm counting on it, because I can't live like this any longer." In truth I died a long time ago.

I lean over the top of her and kiss her in a half upside down move that keeps her pinned to the couch, she doesn't kiss me back but she doesn't resist me either and I know half the battle is won. I stand up behind her the couch separates us and put her knife in my pocket. I want to be closer to her now.

"Get up, Avery and go to the bedroom." She just sits there, unmoving except for the tear that still rolls down her cheek landing on the coloured side of her chest. Half of her is inked, a straight line down the centre front and back divides the two sides of this woman. Detailed art is etched into her skin, hummingbirds, flowers and sugar skulls. The intricate design distracts me a little in that moment I have only seen them from far away before. "NOW!" I yell because the anger has returned, she needs to feel this searing pain that rips me inside.

"You can't do this again, Eiran."

"I can and I will." I grab her soft hair in my fist and drag her up so she knows that I'm going to do this no matter the cost. She reaches for the knife I already removed when I kissed her, a panicked hiss escapes when I drag the blade up to her throat. "Go to the bedroom, Avery. I am not going to ask you again. I'm going to hurt you, how much, depends on you." She turns herself so that I'm faced with those eyes that haunt my sleepless nights.

"I can't feel twice in one day, Eiran, just stop it. I'm breaking and I don't know how to stop it." Her fingers wrap around mine on the knife. "He used this knife to seduce me tonight. I liked it, I liked letting him fuck me, Eiran. I liked being hurt so it is not going to work." Oh, I know this game and she won't win.

"Give up, Avery, because I'm going to have my cock inside you before I die, and we both know I won't be leaving alive tonight. There's just no way on earth that you can't not kill twice in one night." I'm going to hurt your feelings not your body. I turn her away again I can't look anymore I can see the fracture in her composure and it hurts me as much as it does her. I need the rage, the anger, the bubbling I felt after every single clean up. Her bitter words tell me a secret truth and I know just how to break her, wound her and rip that black heart from her chest.

I'm going to love her, something no one else has ever done. I don't even think her father loves her like I do, she has been coached to exclude emotion from everything all her life. Conditioned into a machine so that nothing can break her. Only they failed because she feels things but hides them under the shell of perfection. I'm going to topple the queen. I have to wreck her forever. I'm going to die for her.

AVERY

Better than a thousand hollow words,
is one word that brings peace.

I CANNOT SHUT OFF the sickening feeling that I'm broken. Everything I've practiced for years is failing me. I feel like every single emotion that I have forced below the surface my whole life is coming alive and they're attacking me in the form of Eiran. I know I have to kill him tonight, I need to kill him so I can stop feeling everything he was the one who started the feelings if I kill him they will go away. I need them to go away. My body won't obey my mind and my mind has short circuited with his touch. Eiran said he would rape my emotions and he has done just that, every single loving touch and soft kiss was like having my virginity ripped from me again. It hurt worse this time because he knew exactly what he was doing, he came here with the intention of stealing from me and I am letting him do it again. He doesn't hurt my body like Mathew did, he slaughters my heart with every feather light intentional touch. Physical touch is blurred out by the tearing of my sanity and the pure unfiltered pain of knowing that I have loved him since I was fifteen and I should've killed him then. I kept him because I couldn't let the feeling go completely and now it is here to murder me. Taking my life with his tender words and sucking my soul with his kisses.

His body is like mine. A machine designed for darkness and destruction yet this time I cannot overpower him because I don't want to. Time hazes into noth-

ing and I'm warmed by the sun and I don't care about it, my phone rings contin-
uously from another room but still I don't care. I'm bound to the headboard of
the spare bedroom and Eiran has his face between my legs. My screams silenced
hours ago when I surrendered to his love, when I started to believe the words that
he whispered in my ears. He loves me. I love him. Over and over, he stabbed my
empty fucking heart with his adoration until I felt it start beating. I want it to
fucking stop.

I close my eyes but it does nothing but amplify the feelings that have overtaken
my whole body as I come again. He won't stop, he has yet to put his cock inside
me but I don't think I can take anymore. "Stop please. I don't love you." I try to
sound convincing. I try to make him go away. "Then you can kill me when we are
done, Avery, but I'm not done and you're lying." His words are the opposite of his
actions, hard and cold.

I felt the fear of the truth around my throat strangling me, his hands were
there too but mostly it was fear. I gasped to breathe past it, to bury it with everything else I'm not allowed to feel. I pleaded with my mind to lock this all away,
no air, no breath comes. I want to let it consume and kill me, but I want to kill
Eiran more. His raspy voice in my ear as he finally fucks me unlocks a door that
shouldn't be opened. "Say you love me and I will let you kill me." My back arches
into his body, the pleasure overrides logic. The feelings consume my rationality,
the physical touch has started an emotional flood that cannot be contained. I
want to slip away and float in the waters that it has set free but I cling to what I
know is the truth. Love will kill you. His body becomes a part of me and I want
to push it away but I pull him closer still. I'm dying. "I know you love me, Avery.
I know that you feel me." He continues to torture me. "Admit it, Avery." I can't
admit that I am broken. I can't admit the truth. I won't be a failure.

Then there was a minute where I felt myself leave and I was watching from
the side, I can see my body being worshiped, he fits so perfectly against me. Every
touch designed to make me feel it. Muscles. Scars. The ones I gave him and for the
first time I see my name drawn in script so beautiful you can barely read the words
on his back. 'Avery cut my heart to ribbons with her cold knife of love.' I read
them over and over and over as his movements become more focused and the tip-
ping point of my release is getting closer, my mouth is open and my eyes are about
to roll slightly as muscles start to twitch. A physical response but only this time,
I'm feeling it in another way. I'm up against the wall of my world versus his and
it is breaking under the pressure. The physical release causes a mental separation

and that me and this me become two separate people, she's so strong, she won't ever buckle and break. I have shattered and the shiny pieces of me are floating around the room as I shudder from the orgasm and my mouth lets the surrender slip out of it with words that betray me. "I always loved you, Eiran."

"I know you did, Avery. I can't do this any longer." He climbs off me and the bed. I hear the rip as he cuts the fabric binds from my wrists, the tension is released and I pull my spent naked body to sit up. His eyes are dark, sad and hurt. Ten years he has loved me and I have hurt him. He silently hands me my knife before walking to the bathroom leaving me and all these feelings that have taken the air right out of the room. The silence gives me the space I need to realise that I have always felt this way. Ignoring, hiding and smothering those feelings has been my whole life and I hate it. But right now I hate him more for opening up this giant wound in my mind that I can't even begin to close. I can still hear my phone ringing. It's Callum most likely. I'm about six hours late for work at this point I don't care. I couldn't work today if I tried. The knife is turning sweaty in my grip as I squeeze it, knowing exactly what it's going to be used for now. When I slither from the bed, through the silence I find Eiran laying in the empty bath tub, his phone, gun, lighter and a crumpled picture of me are on the edge of the tub beside him. He has a cigarette hanging from his mouth and his eyes are closed. I take a minute to appreciate the man that has destroyed me. No longer the boy from ten years ago that defined a part of me that can never be changed, he's ripped and muscles line his torso. Beautiful tattoos adorn parts of him that I haven't seen since that day. He's something to behold. My knife marks still visible on his body where I was too weak to kill him the first time, I won't be weak today. "You are taking too long, Avery," he says opening his eyes and a small smile plays on his lips. He knows I'm going to kill him, he's not even going to try and escape the fact. "If you love something kill it, right? I'm waiting. I can die now that I know I didn't imagine what you felt." I step into the tub standing between his legs, all of him on display to me and although all I want is the numb static noise of every other kill, I'm cursed with the burden of sadness as I lean down and push my knife straight through his beautiful cold heart. The feeling of resistance as I try pull it out as if his heart is hanging onto my betrayal and won't let go makes me hesitate. Our eyes are locked and he reaches up to touch my face with his now bloodied hand, tears roll down his cheeks and mine. I'm murdering the only thing I have ever loved, I'm killing myself with him. I slide my hands over his bald head and pull it back exposing his neck to my blade, the blood sprays across me and the whole room as

I finally end the last ten years.

I sit myself down on his corpse and light one of his cigarettes and do something that is so unnatural to me that I feel ill, I cry. Sobbing noises are coming from my mouth as my chest heaves and tears flow, snot blocks my nose and I melt into a mess of the one thing I have tried so hard to avoid—emotion. Feeling is awful I never want to do it again. I turn on the water to drown out the sound of myself.

WHAT FEELS LIKE hours later, I'm still sitting in a pool of blood, above a cold body, blood tears and sex stain my naked body and I realise that there is no one to clean up this mess. I reach for Eiran's phone to call Callum, but I just can't, I dial my father instead.

It rings for ages before he answers. "This is Rowan."

"Dad."

"Avery, who's phone is this?"

"Dad . . ." my words won't come out because I have no idea what to say. I sniff back a new wave of tears.

"I'm coming, baby." He hangs up and I don't need to explain to him, I know he will understand that I'm broken, shattered and worst of all feeling this kill down to my soul. I turn around and lay on Eiran's bloodied chest and stare at my ceiling. My tears and his blood mix and I know he has won in death, he made me feel everything and I cannot switch it off he has raped my soul. I'm bleeding, only there's no blood pouring from me. The exsanguination of my existence happens slowly as I lay in the empty bath tub with my love and consider whether or not to kill myself with his gun? Time stops and nothing exists past the minute I'm in, that time it takes to decide live or die. I have decided it for so many other people over the years it should be second nature, but something in me is clinging to memories of just before Eiran tapped on my car window—Mathew. I'm going to have to kill him too. It is always this way, let someone close enough and you have the worry of getting rid of them after. He set my alarm bells ringing so loud yet I ignored them, I looked for that thrill of danger in him and I got way more than I bargained for. The last twenty-four hours have turned into a shit-storm that I'm not ready to face.

The sound of my front door wakes me. I must have dozed off again and achy exhaustion still drags my body into a groggy numbness stopping my movements.

I just lay still and listen. Door closes, footsteps. Bedroom door opens and closes, click of the handle. Footsteps coming closer to the guest suite, closer to me. I wrap my fingers around his gun and point the loaded weapon at the door. My hand shakes. My hands never shake and I steady it quickly. My nose is still stuffy from crying, I remind myself never to do that again it's horrible. I shake my head searching for my right mind to come back to me, I feel like I have woken up in another person's head. Like I've come back from the dead and I'm not quite the same any more. I see my father and his stare makes me drop the gun. A scream escapes me as a bullet fires and shatters the mirrored wall while dad dives out of the way. Careless mistakes I would never make, what is wrong with me? I feel physically weak, my body is shaking from the cold and something I haven't felt since I was just a kid. Remorse. I'm sorry for something and nothing. I sit up a little, still on top of Eiran and still very naked. "Dad?"

"Get in the fucking shower, Avery." He answers still from around the corner. My dad just saw my boobs—this day can't get worse. My shaky legs lift me from the tub and the ice cold body in it. He no longer looks like a person, just the empty shell of another life I've taken. Usually I leave before they look dead. I stare at him for a minute. "SHOWER, Avery." Another instruction from my father. I don't want to wash his blood from my body but I pad across the floor to the shower that affords me some privacy from the rest of the room. The water is cold at first, making me shake even more as it slowly begins to warm me up and rinse the desperation from my body. "Want to talk about it?" my dad asks now inside the room I hear the rustle of plastic and other objects being brought in.

"I can't." I manage to get the words out before the uncontrollable urge to cry comes over me again.

"Are you okay?" He's standing close now just behind the wall keeping me out of his sight. "Avery?"

"No, Dad. I'm not okay." I tell the truth and slide down to the floor of the shower wishing I could just drown.

"Clean yourself up, you are coming with me back to the estate. I'll go call Callum." He sounds just as distant as always.

I hear muffled voices and my dad arguing loudly with someone as I step out of the shower, Eiran is wrapped in thick industrial plastic and Dad has started to clean some of the blood. The bloody footprints I left are still clear as day across the floor and the shattered shards of mirror shine like the diamonds I loathe so much. I try not to cut my feet as I leave the room in a fluffy towel with my wet hair dripping down my back. Why did he give me the knife? He knew I was going to kill him. The only thing I ever loved is dead in my bathtub. He gave me the knife. Why did he do that? There are people walking about my space, I know them. Cleaners. But I don't want them to clean him, I want to bury him. With mom in the quiet. He is mine, I got to keep him so he is mine even now he is dead.

Inside my bedroom, I dry my body, the tattoos I have kept so carefully hidden for so long seen by my dad, the significance of ink on skin to us is different than to others. He knows why I do it, he does it too. When I was about twelve, he explained the numbers in his heart to me. He told me the story of my how my mother coloured away the scars of her abuse. I didn't know then just what she had lived through, only later in life Callum explained how Renzo had tormented her. Slipping on a pair of jeans and a Motherland band T-shirt, I look at my reflection in the mirror, a twenty-five year old ghost stares back at me. I was never a child, never a teenager, never a young woman I was always this black hole and now it's consuming even the bits of me I was trying to save from the abyss.

"Crocodile farm." I hear my dad bark at someone, my home is crawling with them now. I'm going to have to move, I don't want to but I know I will have to.

"No, Dad!" I yell out from my room.

"Avery, I'm trying to make this go away." He steps into the room and my heart sinks deeper as the cold empty man stares at me with disappointment. I'm an emotional wreck and that's not allowed. I'm letting him down. He doesn't understand me, he doesn't know me and I am scared to tell him what's happening inside me.

"Dad, he's mine please. I want to put him by mom." I sigh, unable to look him in the eye as I ask. He won't like what he sees in my eyes today.

"Avery, what's going on girl?" He walks closer to me. "I have never questioned this strange need to have him around. I never asked why you didn't kill him in that shack, but now I am worried. You're falling to pieces, making mistakes, missing work and killing in your home. So you need to tell me so I can understand why he deserves a place near your mother?" His hands are on my shoulders now as he bends to try and look into my eyes.

"He is the only one who ever made me feel. Anything." His blue eyes search mine for answers I don't have. *"Daddy I don't think I can do this anymore, I loved him and it has broken me." Daddy, oh God Daddy. I'm dying and I need your help I want to beg him to save me but I can't, he can't know how weak I am.*

"Go get in my car, we're going home, baby girl." He is out the door in a blink. I hear him tell them to take Eiran's body to the farm under the cover of darkness tonight and to bury him there. My fear subsides just a little bit and I slip on a pair of ballet flats and go to wait for my dad in the car.

CALLUM

It's a man's own mind, not his enemy or foe that lures him to evil ways.

SOMETHING IS WRONG. I feel it, I have this sense for knowing when things aren't right. I have had her by my side long enough to know when she isn't okay.

I called her all night and she didn't answer, neither did Eiran, but he was so drunk he's probably sleeping it off. My morning coffee tastes like shit and I consider whiskey before nine in the morning again as I glance at my watch for the hundredth time. She's never this late to the office, she never doesn't answer my calls. I dial again, only now her phone's off and my gut sinks as I recall her kidnapping from years before, that's when Eiran entered our little world and her strange killing spree started. She connected to him but never let him close. He became her pet project she had him find a place where she could taunt him. I never tried to understand them but I know enough to know that they are linked by something far deeper than either will ever admit. He's going to be an issue where my plans are concerned. I need their bond broken even if I have to have him killed myself.

The pain is unbearable today and I know I'm already on borrowed time, I'm maxed out on pain meds and it's too early to drink. I buzz the reception desk outside.

"Call my doctor please and have him come in." I'm suddenly reminded he was with her last night, I'll be asking him about that. I don't like their union, albeit a night, there is a plan in place and her liking someone could fuck it all up. Harmon is sitting at my desk trying to absorb all the company information he can in as little time as possible. He is the future, my self-nominated saviour and I have faith in him. Maybe if I keep telling myself that enough times, I'll believe that they can be the formidable force I want them to be. My desk phone rings. The line that is for stuff that no one on earth should know about. It's never good when it rings.

"Callum speaking."

"It's me." Rowan's voice comes back at me and I know instantly something isn't right.

"Where is she?" I ask Rowan because there would be no other reason to call me on this line.

"With me, Callum, something completely fucked up is happening to her and I'm taking her to the farm. She killed Eiran last night." It takes me a moment to register what he said. He sounds tired, he sounds like I feel—beaten. He has a daughter he can't love and he failed her in every way. He has no idea what to do with her, he never did, not when she was born and not now.

"She what?" Oh Eiran you fool I said go home.

"She slept on top of his dead body in her bathtub. Callum, she's fucked up. She needs a break. She cried, you and I both know that isn't okay for her." He tries to explain it to me. None of us will understand her. She is like Shannon there is no understanding them, broken girls are dangerous women.

"I don't have time for her to have a fucking break, Rowan." I snap at him because I don't, time is one luxury I don't have at all.

"Make a plan, Callum. My daughter is coming home with me." His intended meaning is clear she is his not mine. I knew something was wrong, but this is perfectly fine by me, with Eiran out of her way my plans will be easier to implement. I just need her to pull herself back together.

"Fix this, Rowan, fast. Now isn't the time for her to grow a fucking heart." I snap. I'm in pain and I'm irritated.

"She always had a heart, Callum. We made her hide it away remember." The line goes dead in my ear. Fuck.

I slam the phone down and look up to see Harmon looking at me with a smug smirk that I am getting used to now. "Want to talk about it?" he asks me. Do I? "Not really."

"Avery problems? I take it she won't be in for our special meeting today?" He's so full of himself. If I had the strength I would smack him.

"No, we will have to reschedule." I sit down at her desk, what happened to her. She was flawless and now she's a disaster waiting to happen. Where is that fucking doctor? I'm hurting.

"Can you leave for a while?" I ask Harmon to go so I can drink before the pain consumes me. God, dying is almost as hard as living has been, can nothing just go as it should. I silently curse the woman I loved for this punishment. Images of her bruised broken body flash into my head and I'm reminded why it is I'm dying now. I started a war I couldn't win with her. I loved her and didn't kill her before she could kill me. I made a mistake and it has cost me my life. I taught Avery that love would kill her, so did Rowan. I'm a horrible human being, I never claimed to be anything else. A villain was born in my mother's blood and I will die with the same darkness I have lived with. Madness was born in me, just like murder was born into Avery. Sometimes our inheritance isn't worth living for anymore. I have money, power and anything I want in the world but I never found love, not even from the child I raised as my own. Love is reserved for the other people in this world, those that are not like us. Razor blades slice through my side as the pain intensifies leaving me slightly breathless another reminder of just how little time I have left. The office door swishes open as Mathew comes inside, his expressions tells me I look about as shitty as I feel today.

"You look like crap, Callum, it's a bit early to be on the booze isn't it?"

"I'm fucking dying. It's never too early when you are dying. I heard *you* had an eventful night last night." He looks like the cat stole the canary, oh yes Doc, I know everything.

"She told you?" he asks with a slight smile looking around the room to see if she is here somewhere. They had sex, good sex, it's written all over his face and I want to punch him. She wasn't meant for him.

"No, she's having a personal day. You know there's someone watching her all the time don't you?" I smile. I still love playing the games. "Avery has a dirty shadow, nothing she does goes unnoticed, doctor. Watch out where you play. The other guy she fucked last night is dead in a bathtub." He winces a little at the other guy comment. His ego is wounded, he thought he was special, poor fool, no one is special to that girl.

"I just had some fun, I think she did too. She doesn't know it yet but she likes to be pushed around a little." He's trying to make me react so I don't.

"Hmm. Just know what you are getting into, the score is pretty uneven where she is concerned eighty-seven dead bodies and she is still adding to it every week."

I need him to back off, I need her to want Harmon, to need him she has to fucking choose him.

"Callum, Callum? Are you alright?" His voice brings me back to the room.

"No the pain is off the charts today. Like four hundred not ten." I tell him as it slashes at my insides again. "And I have a fucking headache."

"Callum, we need to talk about your plan, now, I'm being honest. There is really very little I can still do for you. You're going to start going into rapid organ failure soon and we wanted to avoid that at all costs." I know what he's saying, time is a bitch just like my wife was.

"I need two days to finalise things then we can do it, Mat, I'll be done. Thursday is the end." He nods as injects me with something to dull the agony but it never does and hands me a joint.

"Smoke it, old man, it will help."

He packs his things meticulously into his bag while I smoke the weed he just handed me and chase it with whiskey. "She liked you," I say out loud, the drugs talking. "Or you'd be very dead already." He frowns at me.

"Avery isn't going to kill me, Callum. Not before I kill you if that's your concern. It was fun, but I rarely go back for seconds and I'm not going to be in town long after Friday." Closing his bag up and looking at me with the pity I loathe, he nods at me. "She is different though, something very special in her." I hear the evil undertone and the angel of death twinkles in his eye. The darkness inside him likes the pitch black inside her, they are a dangerous combination.

"I suggest you leave her alone, Mat. I have her future very well planned out and you, my boy, are not in it." My threat clear he gives me a knowing nod one villain to another. There's a reason I don't trust doctors, Shannon, him and countless others in between. They're evil fuckers all of them. We talk about my plan for the future as I get high and the sweet smoke takes my pain away. I need him to know she has a future all mapped out.

"See you Thursday, Callum. Take it easy. I'm looking forward to it. Don't ruin my fun." The slimy fuck leaves me to smoke, drink and wrap up my business and my life.

There is nothing else for me, no redemption and forgiveness doesn't come for those who are born damned, so I'm happy knowing I will not be going to a better place. I don't deserve one, I'm not nor have I ever been worthy of anything good, my life is a testament to that. I'm a living breathing tragedy and I will suffer the tragic end I deserve, but I will do it on my terms and in my time. The only thing

I will keep in this world is the sliver of dignity that I have hung onto through this disease. I sit at my desk and sign my new will and testament, the one that splits my assets between Avery and Harmon should he honour his appendix to the contract within two years of the date of signing. Should he not do so his half goes to my sister Amya. I may not live to see it but I can die in the hope that my dream of a suitable successor will come true. Slipping the notarised documents back in the envelope, I get up to go and deliver them to my lawyers on the third floor as Harmon is coming back into the office. He's a twenty year younger version of me, without a death sentence tightening around his neck, regret sneaks into my mind as I think of all the things I would have done differently. There aren't many, the biggest one is I would never have shoved the girl who held my heart out of her bedroom window. My path was changed that night more than any other of the defining moments that came before or after, that night left my feelings exposed. That night turned me into a vicious rapist. It tipped me over the edge and started a free fall into madness that I still cannot stop. Once upon a time, I was just a boy with a gun in his hand and the desperate need to belong in the world. Now I'm a sad, bitter old man with an empty heart and home and I'm too weak to hold a gun to kill myself.

I stop Harmon in the middle of the reception area holding out my hand, I shake his. "It's up to you and her now. I'm done. Try not to fuck it all up at once." He looks confused like he really thought I would be here longer, but also like he has no idea what to say to me at all. "Bye, Harmon." I let his hand fall and walk away from everything I have built with the blood of my family.

AVERY

All wrong-doing arises because of mind. I
f mind is transformed can wrong-doing remain?

ON MONDAY NIGHT, I felt something. On Tuesday, I killed the one person I think I might have loved. On Wednesday, I woke up in my childhood room with tears burning my cheeks. On Thursday, I saw my father's eyes as he cried and tried to tell me the news that Callum died. On Friday, I sat between the graves of my mother and dead lover. I wished for the little girl that used to swing in the tree that is now burnt and fallen to come back and breathe her life into me. On Saturday, I couldn't get out of bed and Sunday, I drowned in the wine from the vineyard store. On Monday, I got dressed but never left for work, my dad tried to talk to me and I cried, so he left. In a week, I have lost everything that held me together and as I fall apart slowly and painfully I don't even try and keep any part of me I let it all shatter and break apart.

TODAY IS FRIDAY AGAIN and we stand in the little graveyard like we used to on Sundays. Dad and me and a lady I think I remember but cannot place. She's beautiful and her skin is covered like my dad's while a big man holds her hand as she wipes her cheeks with an old fashioned hanky. Callum's half-brother, Harmon is here, we met once—he's a dick. The Catholic priest drones on and I don't listen to a word of the drivel that he spews. Callum didn't believe he was going to heaven anyway, he was comfortable with the fact his soul couldn't be saved. My tears have dried up again, I don't like to cry and the last week has made me hate it. Everyone has tears except for me and Harmon, he seems to hate crying too by the way he looks at them all. I'm fascinated. He looks so much like Callum, only his eyes are amber not green and he isn't frail or wrinkled, he's strong and young. He even dresses just like the old man, the signature O'Reilly three piece suit even when it's as hot as hell out. Over twenty years I never once saw Callum in anything else. My dad wears jeans, he is sort of old school cool with his ink and greying hair and beard. Even now he has jeans on, he doesn't change who he is for anyone—ever. I see a shadow behind the remains of the tree I used to swing in as child, standing away from the few who cared is the doctor that started this spiral into mayhem for me. I swallow a very heavy realisation—he killed Callum. No, Callum asked him to die before it got too bad. He killed him, the anger starts to bubble even though I know he wouldn't have had a choice with Cal, he did it and I hate him for it. I try to stand still as the sharp acid of my rage starts to burn inside me. I shuffle my feet and look at my dad next to me, he grabs my hand and squeezes it. When I look up again Mathew's gone, but I will find him. I drop the single white Arum Lily onto the coffin as I step right next to the gaping hole in the ground and it swallows up part of my soul as they fill it in.

It turns out the beautiful lady is Callum's sister, Amya. She was around when I was a baby and even took care of me, I remember her face but nothing else. The big man with her is her husband Robin. They all laugh and tell stories of Callum and my mom and how Robin was the one who did all their tattoos, before he left no one else had drawn on my dad. Cupcakes, wine and café stories that couldn't sound less like Callum if they tried, the Callum I knew was different. He was the man who killed the devil, ruthless, loveless, cold, calculated and above all lonely, but he gave me the attention my father wouldn't. We all sit on the patio and drinking and eating, Harmon's silent almost the whole time, I don't think he really knew his brother at all besides a few phone calls. I'm not sure they had anything to do with each other. I feel his eyes boring into me and as the sun starts to sag close to the horizon I can't bear anymore of this and I excuse myself to my room. I close my door and kick off my shoes, a shower is what I need. I cannot face a bathtub yet, as much as I would love to soak in one I just can't get Eiran's dead body out of my head.

When I emerge from the bathroom, my dad's sitting in the chair by the window looking out at the vineyard and the almost night sky that isn't dark or light. "Want to talk about it yet, kid?" he asks and I think I might want to but I am not sure I can.

"About what, dad?" I ask softly because truth is I have no idea where to start, I was closer to Callum than him because he shut me out. Dad was detached, he taught me to kill, that was our connection, but there was nothing more. The deep bond that should be shared between parent and child was missing.

"All of it if you want."

"You remember when I was kidnapped and I came home with Eiran?" He doesn't turn and face me which is better really, I think I might just spill some very ugly truths not even he is ready for. Looking into his tragic eyes will make it harder.

"I remember, you changed after that. Killing became easy for you." He's right, it did. It no longer felt like work, but became a release for the insanity inside me, I wanted to love Eiran instead I killed.

"He raped me, not one of you even asked me if I got hurt because I filleted him, you all thought I was fine. I cut a man apart and you all thought I was fine." My Dad's back goes ramrod straight and stiffens where he no stands up his hands pressed against the windows.

"Worst part of it was how much I liked it, how he made me feel. He made me feel a little tickle under the hard shell that you and Callum made me wear. I fell in love with the boy that stole my virginity, then I spent ten years torturing him by fucking other men and killing them so he had to clean up, dad. Still want to talk about it?" He nods I can only see the back of his head and a reflection of his face in the glass, he was always just a reflection of his loss.

"Eighty-seven dead bodies and not once did you or Callum try to stop me. At least Callum would yell and scream and make me feel like I should try not to. You never uttered a word." I take a minute to let the things I'm saying sink in for both of us, facing truths like these isn't always easy. My father didn't care enough to try stop me from being a heartless murderer.

"You hide here on this farm and come out of your little hole only when you have to. You don't see me—the real me, the fucking disastrous mess you and Callum made." His head drops to his chest in honest defeat. I feel my fingernails digging into my palms as I catch my breath after yelling at him. Panting for breath I hunch myself over and close my eyes.

"I failed you, Avery, you don't think I know that? You don't think I look at your mother's picture and see all the broken promises and shattered fucking dreams. I could not love you." His voice is soft and sad and his head hangs down his shoulders now rounded over and hunched. There it is, the L word, the forbidden feelings.

"I loved Eiran, so I killed him. You want to know who taught me that?" I wait a second to see if he answers me. "Callum, because other than how to commit a flawless murder you taught me nothing about life, about how damn hard it is to be human."

"I'm sorry, Avery." His words are soft and they hurt me so much I yell back.

"Sorry? You don't get to be sorry, Dad." I slump down onto my bed and stare at his reflection. I don't want an apology I wanted a dad.

"I am done, I don't want his empire, I don't want to run your murder mill and I certainly don't want to keep being a shell. I felt something the night I killed Eiran, not with him. Someone else made me feel and my God it was so good. I want to be allowed to be angry, hurt, tired, sad, bitter, happy and fuck it all I would like to know is that someone in this rotten filthy world loved me at some point. I am done, Dad. Done." He turns around now, I can see the shine of a tear on his cheek, he is human he feels things. He feels them bone deep just none of them are good things. Why am I not allowed the same privilege, why am I banned from having my heart broken?

"I don't think you have a choice. Being done isn't an option for people like us, Avery."

"People like us? Just say it, Dad. MURDERERS. That's what we are. Stone cold killers." The acidic rage eats me from the inside out as I spew angry words at him.

"You need to pull yourself together. I know I came in here and asked to talk to you, but I am done talking now. You want to be done? Try it and see what happens." He shoves his hands in his pockets as he walks right up to me.

"And Avery, I tried being done once, your mother hated me for it. She hated herself for it and I can promise, you will hate it. This is your birthright not a career day expo. It is in you and there is no getting it out." I know it's there, I feel it inside me and I want to purge myself of the curse born in me.

I stare at myself in the windows a murky reflection. I have two faces, one of them I am not and the other is a murderer. Neither of them is who I want to be. I fall asleep with my demons playing over and over in my head and I wake to them in my home. My ringing phone wakes me, I don't want to answer it but I do because the other option is talking to Dad again and that was agonising enough the first time.

"Ms Leahy, are you planning to come into work sometime this month?" The thick Irish accent has a hint of Callum in it makes my heart stops for a minute.

"Unless I died and someone made you the boss, I can't see how it is any of your business Mr . . ."

"O'Reilly and Callum died and made us co-bosses so I sort of need you to show up eventually." Harmon, the dickhead. I missed the reading of the will because I didn't really care about what Callum gave to who, I don't need his money. The devil that killed my mother left me all of his.

"Fuck off." I hang up. Today isn't the day for this. I pour wine into a coffee mug and drag myself to the patio where I watch the vines dance in the wind and breathe the air of the valley morning in. The house is eerily quiet this morning and my Dad has obviously left. Something he doesn't do often so I am wondering what was so urgent now, but I know he is just hiding from me. I'm hungry, for the first time in over a week I actually want something to eat. The kitchen is one place I felt my mother, I may have never known her but in here she still lives and breathes. Right in the middle of the island is a small pile of envelopes with my name on them and a sticky note with Dad's writing.

It's time you read these.
x Dad

There is one new envelope on top so I start there. I don't want to think about what was in the letters now, maybe later when I'm ready to face the things that will be revealed. One was from Callum and the other three were from my mother. I took the letters, a small bag of clothes and my work bag of guns and knives and I left. I am using my escape plan. I got on the N1 and drove, away from Cape Town away from my life and away from myself because I hate myself. Every kilometre that passed, I felt the freedom. I never realised I craved it as I feel it filling the empty cavity that the events of the last two weeks had made. I shed the spiky skin of my upbringing and embrace the idea of being someone new, I can be anyone I create now. I still haven't eaten but the sickness in my stomach wouldn't let me eat now. My father had those letters for me, all my fucking life he had the chance and never gave them to me. I'm so angry at him.

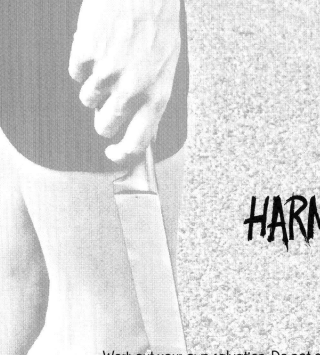

HARMON

Work out your own salvation. Do not depend on others.

AT FIRST I WASN'T worried at all when Avery didn't show up to the reading of the will, or work or anything at all. I heard she killed some guy that had been around for years and that she has had a breakdown and is staying with her father. At first I thought oh well two years is plenty time to seduce her into my bed and have my offspring in her belly. But now I am worried, two years isn't that long and Avery Spillane-Leahy has disappeared off the face of the earth. Callum's agreement is iron clad, even I can't find a fucking loophole—yet. I have got to find her she has had her fun, three months of it and I'm not a patient person. I also need to enlist some help or get some friends in this shithole place because I have no idea what I am doing and everyone in here is treating me like the enemy outsider.

To be honest, I thought Callum was a lunatic and I still think he had gone a bit mad from the disease and the medication, the office smelled like fresh pot the day he walked out. Now I have had time to mull it over, the families tried this once before to bring things together with a marriage and a child, he was that child, but the old world thinking and stubborn men couldn't let it be. Now there is none of that mob mentality. This is a business and a merger would make sense, the girl owns half the Italian mob interests by some default deal and her name, well names still hold a weight of power with crime circles all over the world. Together we would be a formidable opponent for anyone who tried to topple us and they will try. The king has fallen, the queen doesn't want a crown. We are vulnerable and open to be attacked. Callum foresaw this and that's what his plan was about, my brother had a brilliant mind and no conscience that is why he succeeded even in death he was planning the future.

I've managed to make one friend in my attempts to run this enterprise and find the missing Avery, a diamond dealer. Sam, it seems was as close as a friend that Avery had. According to him she doesn't do people, friends or family. Well that doesn't help me much, she has also killed eighty-seven men after having sex with them the cleaning team here divulged that much. They told me that bodies are bound to start showing up wherever she has gone and I should just wait for them to get the call to clean, three months and not one. She either stopped killing, or got exceptionally good at hiding the bodies.

I'm slowly unravelling the intricate web of the company though, weapons, diamonds, drugs, people and any other illegal merchandise you can think of come through us, like a hub of evil. The port here is owned almost exclusively by us, it's perfectly central to move things all over the continent and the world. We make our money trading one for the other in and out, raw diamonds in, and polished cut ones out. Drugs out and sex slaves in to be moved to other parts of the world. Stolen women out and arms in, it really is ingenious that way the place is structured. We have the gangs on the streets, pushing drugs, kidnapping girls and buying guns. And every sector of business from there on up has some tie to us, this city is the filthiest place ever. Corrupted and bought by the blood of many, I've fallen in love with it already. We even own the police and politicians. It is easy to be a criminal here, I understand the reason Callum chose it and there will never be peace so no one has the time to see the clean crime that is happening under all the violence.

I pick up the phone, every day I try.

"Rowan, it's Harmon, is Avery there? Have you heard from her?" I ask him, but I think he's happy she's gone so he never actually helps me. He's an odd man, deadly, but quiet and observant. He is reclusive and secretive about everything, he never says one word more than he has to.

"No and no, Harm. Let it go just take the business and run it yourself. She said she was done." She doesn't get to be done, yet.

"Thanks, Rowan." He hangs up, I get the feeling he doesn't like to be bothered. He hides on that farm and never leaves. I wonder why Callum was so protective of him, he guarded Rowan like he was the only thing that mattered.

I have a team of investigators looking for my lost girl and I have this feeling that she isn't far away just really good at hiding away. I will find you, little hummingbird and when I do you are going to be sorry you have wasted my time. A knock on the door just makes my mood worse, "Come in." I bark.

"Hi." It's Sam in his high pitched fake queer voice that makes me grind my teeth.

"Hi, Sam," I sigh out taking my glasses off and shutting down the computer screen so he can't see what I am doing.

"Want to go for lunch?" It cannot be lunch time already. I look at my watch and true as god it's eleven thirty.

"Sure why not. Where we going?" I don't share his vegan hippie tastes in food so I am always afraid of what the answer will be. I'm vegetarian some stupid rule Callum made years ago, but there is no way I'm eating some of the shit they come up with.

"I want to take you somewhere. A surprise. And it's not vegan." He winks, great a surprise I plaster a fake smile on my face and put my jacket back on.

"I'll drive." I just don't like his pansy little hairdresser car.

"Let's go." He's so annoying but the only ally I have so I put up with his drivel and weirdness. I think he puts most of it on to upset his father.

We get into my car in the underground parking, a sensible SUV with bulletproof windows. I am prepared for the war that will come.

"Head into old town." I look at him like he has gone mad. And he sighs and enters an address into the GPS.

"I think you'll love this. A little history lesson for you." He seriously underestimates my tolerance for crap, but today any escape from the closing walls of that office will suffice.

I blindly follow the talking GPS lady in my dashboard through the traffic and buildings, I haven't been to this part of the city. Sticking to the places close to home, work and the beach has worked just fine so far, I do not feel safe here. I see people living in tents on sidewalks and beggars at every robot or stop street, the urban rot is evident all around me. "You have reached your destination." The voice says as we stop opposite a giant pink building. I must look confused because Sam chimes in at that moment.

"Park in there." He points to a lot that looks like I will get mugged and raped in.

"What is this place, Sam, really?"

"Charly's, Avery loves it and I heard that Callum used to come here with his cousin before, well you know before his wife."

"But what is it Sam?" I look at the building amongst the rotting surroundings and I cannot understand why he has brought me here.

"It's a bakery you nob. Don't you watch the old re-runs on telly. Charly's bakery, cake boss?"

"Unlike you, I am not gay, Sam. I'm also a very busy man." I haven't even turned the television in my home on yet. He laughs and shakes his head at me.

"You need to get laid and learn how to have some fun, Harmon, because if you don't this place will eat you alive." I don't have time for fun and I would love to get laid, but I am too distracted with finding the one woman I have to fuck that finding any others hasn't been a priority.

"I will take you out somewhere fun and full of girls . . . or guys if you like?"

"I like women, Sam. Not girls." I answer as we enter the giant pink box. The place is wall to wall cupcakes, cookies and sugar. Not exactly the lunch I had in mind. Sam has the look of a child in the toy store on his face as his eyes rake over every single delicious treat displayed for us.

"Chose something, Harmon," he says over his shoulder as he picks out something that should be called sugar coma. The only thing that catches my eye are the small petit fours in bright colours displayed behind a glass divider. I order two and a coffee since whiskey isn't an option here and Sam and I sit outside at a small table that has seen better days.

"This place has been here like forty years still makes the best fucking cupcakes on earth," he mumbles with a mouthful of cake.

"What do you want from me, Sam?" I ask because the guy is honestly too nice and it worries me.

"Truth?" He raises an eyebrow.

"No, lie to me. Of course the truth."

"I thought you were gay at first, actually I was hoping you were. You dress like you are." He shoves more cake in his mouth while I decide whether or not to be offended by his statement. I dress like a person, not a hoodlum. Being a criminal means looking like a gentleman always. My father taught me that before Callum had him killed.

"Now, I just kind of like having someone to spend time with." He's being sincere with me, but I'm not sure how to respond. I never had friends. My fiancé

Minnie was the closest thing to a friend I had and she was a money hungry whore.

"Okay." It's the only answer I can manage.

"Okay, well you are nicer than her you know." I have heard she was a bitch. I know the little interaction we had was never pleasant. "Let's go out tonight, maybe I can help you get laid. Women like gay men these days." He winks at me.

"Sam, is being gay a rebellion against your father or something you always felt?" I don't know why but he seems unconvincing in his convictions.

"Both, but mostly too many girls broke my heart and one boy managed to undo all of that hurt after that, well after that I never looked at women again." He's drinking rice milk which is just odd to me. "I guess, Harmon, I go both ways but I do love that going this way upsets my father so very much." I spoke with his father once who was not a nice guy. I never had a father to piss off as teenager, I upset Callum a few times but he was too far away for it to really matter at all.

"Makes sense. Your dad is a bit of a dick." Sam laughs very loudly.

"A bit." He shakes his head still laughing "Let's go, Harmon, I will meet you at the office after work." He looks me over with his fingers pinching his chin. "You have other clothes don't you." He points and waves his finger around at me.

"Other suits, yes."

"No, no suits. Clothes?" He seems horrified.

"No."

"Well don't wear your jacket." We get back in my car and get lost numerous times on the way back to the office.

"Sam, where do you think she went?"

"Avery didn't actually like me, you know that right? She never ever divulged anything personal ever. I only know what she did for fun because she murdered a mutual friend and occasionally hung out at a jazz bar I frequent." It seems she really did have no one in her life at all. I know that bitter bite of loneliness at the end of the day and it sucks.

"I want to go there tonight." It is a long shot, I don't think she's in the city.

"Sure, we can go there. But I can't promise you'll get laid if we do, it's not that kind of place." He can be very juvenile. He goes straight to his car and I head upstairs to face whatever else has managed to cross over my desk in the last two hours.

One of my investigators is waiting when I get upstairs, my heart jumps, maybe they found her?

"Come in." Opening my office door for him I give the nosy girl at the front desk a death glare. I hate them all.

"Tell me you have something for me?" I sit down behind my desk with hope.

"I think I've got her. One of my guys saw a woman matching her description, you know those eyes." Those eyes are unique. I nod for him to go on.

"She's in the Eastern Free State, if it is her. A small town near the Lesotho border post. Has a man with her." He sits forwards a little, leans his elbows on my desk. "What do you want us to do?"

"Nothing. I need an address, and I want surveillance on her. Don't get caught." I remove an envelope of cash from my bottom drawer and hand it to him. Found you, Hummingbird.

"Yes, sir." He leaves my office closing the door behind him.

It is time to play catch. I need to make her come home, I don't want to have to kidnap her I will if I have to but there are other ways to make her return home. There is no out of this family.

AVERY

No matter how hard the past, you can always begin again.

I DON'T KNOW WHERE I'm going to go, I just know that I cannot stay. I stopped in Paarl and withdrew a large sum of cash from the Baldini trust account, not many know about it so by the time they look there, I'll be gone. It's the first time I'd touched the money from my mother's murderer, I always felt it was tainted, not that any of my other money isn't but this always seemed different. Now seems as good a time as any to spend his filthy money. By the time I reach Beaufort West, my car is dangerously low on fuel and I pull into the big 1-Stop. It's bustling with cars and people. I fill the car first then go inside the convenience store to get coffee and something edible to take with me. I'm also dying to pee, just the thought of the public loo gives me the willies but a girl can't hold it forever and if I had to sneeze now it would cause a flood. The shop bustles with families, truck drivers and drifters from all over, the unofficial stop over point on the road to Cape Town this place is always busy. There's a line in the ladies, I can't wait, I slip into the door to the men's room and slink into the nearest stall. Oh the relief as I empty my strained bladder is amazing. I just sit for a second after I'm done. I bury my head in my hands and wonder just what the fuck it is I'm doing? I should just turn around and go back now, what do I know about being off on my own? I have been micromanaged by Callum and my father my whole life. Freedom is scaring the shit out of me. I convince myself the shakes are from hunger and fatigue but when I stand and shudder, the itch to just murder someone is there again, a way to release what I'm feeling. I open the latch and peek out to make sure I don't interrupt some scary trucker type mid piss, you can't unsee things. When I'm satisfied there's no one at the urinal, I push the door open and start to escape from the little boy's room. As I push the exit door I hear footsteps behind me and I try to move faster, but they don't stop. I'm not looking back, just get out and go get coffee that's the plan. Before I can get to the end of the passage the footsteps have gained on me and a man steps right next to me, "Hello, Avery. Are you going somewhere?" Him, it's him. I know it just from the way he said my name and I can smell him. He smells like an Armani advert in mens health magazine. "Hello Mathew, or whatever your name really is. I wouldn't tell you if I was going somewhere."

"Running then?" Who is this man? "From something or to something?" I stop and glare at him as he steps in front of me just a little, his smile is friendly as he lifts an eyebrow genuinely waiting for me to answer him.

"No idea where or why I'm going, Not Mathew, but I needed to leave." I answer him with a half truth, I know why I am running I just have no clue where.

"Have coffee with me before you disappear?" he holds out a hand to me, I nod but don't take it, my body did stupid things the last time he touched me and I'm not letting that happen again. I shove my hands into my pockets, so I'm not tempted to touch him.

"Where are you going, Mathew?" I ask as we re-enter the busy front of the building.

"The next job, I really am a doctor." He says it convincingly enough, I'm reminded that he killed Callum, the one person that kept me from self-destruction was gone and this man took him from me.

"I know you killed him." He glares at me glancing around to see if anyone heard me.

"Sit," he pulls out a chair at the Wimpy for me. "Firstly that's what Callum hired me to do, it was my job to end it before he lost the last shred of dignity he had." A waitress approaches us so he stops talking and we order coffee. He looks pissed at my accusations, the dangerous glint is back in his eyes and I know I've struck a nerve.

"Dying is bad enough without suffering, Avery, we don't even let animals suffer. We save them the agony and put them to sleep. He chose me because I understood that. I was not just a doctor to him, I was his friend we talked, laughed and even fucking drank together. It is not easy what I do you know." He sounds angry and bitter over it. "He spoke about you all the time, he was angry about the other night and told me that I was not in the future he planned for you." Callum was so concerned with the future, he forgot to live before he died.

"I can only imagine, no one was ever part of his plan for me." It is the truth I don't think Callum would ever have approved of anyone if I had let one live long enough to meet him.

"He loved you, Avery, spoke about you all the time." Fool.

"People like us don't love, he needed me. There is a big difference. Love is a very dangerous thing that has no room in our lives, if you love something it has the ability to kill you, break you and change you." He smiles at me as he sips the hot black coffee in his cup.

"The old man loved you dearly, Avery and he used those words. You had the ability to hurt him so it must be love then." I want to stab him with a fork for being right, because that sentiment hurts me. I didn't love Callum, I respected and admired him, but love was never a part of it.

"He told you about what I do then?" I wonder how many secrets Callum spilled, I really should kill him now.

"You are the Hummingbird, an assassin, you are in charge of diamond and gem trade at O'Reilly International. And you are the world's biggest bitch." He drinks more coffee and I can't help but admire him, the way his shirt hugs onto his chest showing off what I already know asunder it. "Oh and you murdered every single person you ever fucked bar one, but I understand you killed him recently too so that makes me the new exception to the rule." He smiles like it's a prize he won, that panty melting smile.

"The day's not over. I might still kill you." I don't like how accurate he is, I don't like that I still don't want to kill him. I hate how my mind is turning the image of him drinking coffee against me and making me remember what that mouth did to me. I'm staring at him, all of him and I like what I see more every minute, he knows who I am, yet he still sits here with me, is that because he is a killer too? He's a stranger yet he sees me. I remember the way he trailed my knife down my naked skin, the way his mouth set my skin alight. Fuck me. He did something to me that disarmed me completely. I tense my muscles to try and stop the pulse between my thighs, there's no denying the fact that my body wants him.

"I will do it again if you want." He snaps my mushy brain back to reality.

"What?" I must have missed something he said.

"Whatever it is you were just remembering as you eye-fucked me, I will do it again." I choke on my coffee and it comes out my nose, I grab at the paper serviettes to try and clean it before it goes anywhere else I still can't swallow what's in my mouth.

"You may not live this time." I answer once the coffee shower is cleaned and I can swallow.

"No one lives forever, Avery, the trick is to enjoy it while you do." Enjoy it? I have never really enjoyed anything in my life. It's a lie. Eiran, I enjoyed that afternoon, those few minutes of real feelings. Even the brutal reality of losing my virginity was over powered by the intense desire for human contact. I enjoyed the way he touched me. I enjoyed Mathew too, which leads me to think I might be falling into a dangerous trap yet again. I need touch, the feel of another person against my skin. I was deprived as a child. My father never hugged me, or held me and neither did Callum, now I crave that touch like a crack addict looking for a fix.

"Where are you going?" I try to change the subject to get my mind to focus away from feeling. I need to find the girl that could switch it off, the one that I was before Eiran and again after him. The one that didn't feel the inconsolable loss of losing Callum slowly over eight fucking years. I felt his death from the second he got ill and I still feel it now, the knowledge of his slow murder made me fear letting anyone close. If the love of his life could be that malicious then love can't be worth it, he once told me he should have killed her the minute he saw her and I get that same feeling now as I look at the handsome doctor.

"To work." He puts his coffee cup down and looks at me with a shit eating grin on his face. "Want to come?"

"Since we both know you are going nowhere." God he's good, good but dangerous and my mind says no and my body says yes and my heart says fuck it all to hell.

"Where's work?" I'm entertaining the idea. Someone drops a glass behind me I hear the pieces shattering all over the floor but I don't turn to look.

"Clarens, a little place where no one will have the faintest idea who you are." It even sounds appealing.

"Why would I go?" I have lost my ever-loving mind.

"Why not? Have you got something better to do?" He has a point. He continues before I can answer. "You do know that they will look for you." He waves his hand at the waiter for the bill. He has a very valid point. The slightly tired looking guy goes to print out our check. I open my mouth and ignore everything I have ever been taught.

"Okay. Bum fuck nowhere it is." He smiles like he just won the lotto and I know I'm making a stupid decision but while I'm on a roll, I may as well go with it, what is one more dumb choice at this point.

"Leave that very obvious car here with the keys in it before you get seen." Leave my car, is he nuts?

"You can get a new one later." My eyes must have given away the horror of it. He's right, I'll be noticed in the bright red sex on wheels.

Mathew pays for the coffee, which irks me a little and I go to empty my car. I'm traveling light so it's my bag of clothes and my *work* bag. I leave my keys in the ignition and walk away from my car and my life and straight towards a murdering doctor and his dog that has its head out of the car window. Just another reminder of the things I was never allowed. I stop for a minute and stare at just how normal he seems on the outside the whole package, dog and all. There's a mountain bike on the back of his SUV, he's leaning against the car next to it watching me. I still have no idea who he really is and to be honest I no longer care, everyone is hiding something and knowing the truth isn't always the best thing. And I will still bet my life his name is not Mathew.

"Let's go." He opens the passenger door for me, all gentleman like. I know you really aren't that guy. "This is Jameson, he farts and barks," he says slipping into the driver's side and petting the dog that has its head stuck between us. I laugh and pet the dog that just looks at me with weary eyes.

"Hi, Jameson." I watch my car and essentially my life in the rear view mirror. He's giving me an out, but for the first time, I fear what this out will bring. My self-preservation and own brain scream that this is a horribly bad idea. The reason I choose to follow, the thrill. I start to think about it and panic, I look at the locked door and the dog and the fear starts to claw from my belly up my throat. I feel the sweat on my palms and the cold feverish feeling spreading over my body. I try to open the window and it won't go at first. I see him unlock it and I open it all the way down letting the wind take my breath from me. Jameson dives on top of me from the back seat giving me a fright. He just wants to stick his head out like me. I let him sit on me and we breathe together, he is heavier than I imagined a dog to be.

CLARENS IS BEAUTIFUL, like take your breath away beautiful, and old and quaint and really small. We're staying on his patient's property a small way outside of town, two small houses and nothing but acres and acres of open nothingness in front of us and a mountain looms behind us. It's cold here and the winter has turned everything to shades of yellow and brown. The news predicted snow in the surrounding mountains so I know it's only going to get worse. In my silly head, I got into his car and we were driving off into the sunset to be a happy couple somewhere but in truth it has been very different. He never said much on the thirteen hour drive to get here, only where we were staying and that he would be here six months to a year. Jameson was better company then Mathew. As we drove, the dog sat on me and comforted my inner demons trying to escape. When we arrived, Mathew went on with his new patient and left me alone in this little house isolated from the outside world and didn't so much as open the car door for me. The cold indifference bothered me but I never said a word, he made no promises only asked if I wanted to go with him. I'm an idiot.

Jameson and I walk every morning along the edge of where the mountain touches the small lake and in the shadows and freezing cold air, I begin to examine myself on the inside. Self-reflection is something I've never really done. Sitting on a rock looking at the open space, I remember another space one that was so small.

"Your ransom will be very high." Eiran's voice taunted me as he sat in front of the chair *I'd been taped to. "I can pay you the ransom money now if you let me go."* I spit answers back at him, because I know they want money and I doubt Callum will notice I'm gone never mind pay it. And my father is out of the country killing someone. I can take care of myself though. I have been taught that from the time I was born. *"We will see you are a pretty girl aren't you."* He leant down and kissed me, not like the cold peck on the cheek from Callum every morning. There was a fire in his kiss and it felt so warm and so good. His lips were on mine and I felt his tongue inside my mouth and I didn't want him to stop. *"Hmm."* He looked at me with eyes that told me how to win this fight and get out of here alive but I would have to give him a part of me.

Jameson barking like a mad fool draws me back and the morning is becoming brighter around me. I see the mist begining to clear, the dog doesn't like the wildlife and he is having a standoff with a duck of sorts. "Come, Jameson." I call him as I jump off the rock and start the walk back to the small stone house. I have been here two weeks, I left my phone in my car so I have no idea what's happening in the world I've run from and as lonely as this one is, it is still not the desolate hate and I had been living in for so long. When I get back, it's one of the rare mornings where Mathew or Not Mathew as I call him, is now home, something in me snaps when I see him in the small kitchen with coffee in his hand and walk straight up to him. I came with him for a reason and to be ignored and walk the dog was not that reason. I step into his personal space and take his mug in my hand, I put it on the counter behind him, and there's a smile on his face. His dark eyes are shining and he licks that lip. He shaved off his beard and his clean smooth face makes him look younger, less intimidating. He just stands there, so I get closer again, my body is against his and I kiss him, I need to feel something and he made me feel before. I don't know how else to get the feeling I need so desperately to save myself from imploding. Mathew kisses me back, his hands pulling me closer still, our tongues touching and this time it is something more than before. His mouth on mine makes me want to cry, scream and kill him, but worse it makes me want more, more of him than just a kiss.

He pulls me away by the hair and I struggle for air from the sharp pain. "I was waiting for that, what took so long?" He's smiling like he's relieved and yet there is a deep hunger in his eyes. I feel like I have found the thing that has always been missing from my life. For the first time since the day Callum returned to our lives I feel everything, sadness, fear, pain, and even if it is only from the dog I feel love. I feel wanted for me and not for the purpose I serve. "Why were you waiting?" I ask leaning against his chest.

NOT MATTHEW

Time does not heal everything but acceptance will heal everything.

I HAVE THIS UNSTOPPABLE need to save people, even when that means helping them die or saving them from themselves. Avery needs to be saved from herself, had I left and never seen her again it wouldn't have bothered me as much, but I saw when they buried Callum. Something in me wouldn't let me leave. When I saw her standing there, not shedding even a single tear, I knew what I'd already suspected that night was true. That girl was going to kill herself if no one saved her. The crowd of soulless, merciless monsters around her certainly were not going to. I didn't interfere. Callum's threat a few days before he passed was stuck in my head, I left just like I had planned to, well around a week later than planned. Jameson and I climbed into my car and drove off towards the Eastern Free State where my next patient was waiting on me, she is an old lady that lives on a large piece of land out there, no children, no family just her. Those are the saddest ones, the ones where literally no one cares if they live or die, the cancer usually takes them faster than those who have family to fight for. At least the dog will like it where we are going plenty of space to run around and animals to chase, the spaniel belonged to a patient and when the old pigeon hunting man passed on, I somehow got stuck with the dog. I don't hunt so Jameson is now a bored lazy dog that gets into trouble often. At Beaufort West, I need to stop so both him and I can both take a piss and refuel.

While I walk him on the small 'pet' lawn at the 1-stop service station, I see a familiar little red sports car buzz past us and scream to a halt in the parking area. I can't stop my heart from skipping as Avery slips out of the car, she looks lost. Her long hair isn't sleek and groomed. It's loose and matted, her mascara is smudged and in place of patent heels, she has on simple flats. She looks so beautifully broken, she looks like I was meant to save her. I put Jameson back in the car, he isn't allowed in the building because he is most certainly not a guide dog, he's a menace. "Stay boy," I say to the head sticking out of the open window searching for something to bark incessantly at and I go inside. My eyes scan the place for her, but I can't see her and nature is calling in the worst way so I go to the men's room as quickly as I can. Not a fan of public displays of penises, I slip into a stall and do my thing. Hoping she hasn't left already, although she looked tired and in need of coffee. Exiting the stall, I get the view of her behind retreating from the men's room, sneaky little minx. I get the feeling that no one has ever bothered to set rules for her and having no boundaries has made her weak. We all have to have a set of rules we live by but that girl is on the path to self-destruct because she has never had any. I walk a little faster to catch up to her, I'm drawn to her because she needs to be saved. I can save her, or at least I can try. Flashbacks of her pinned to my bed as I fucked her into submission, make me walk even faster. She's running away and I'm going to make her run to me.

She was so easily swayed, so unbelievably stupid and naive for someone so versed in being a criminal. She just left it all and came with me. I know that in her fractured mind—where reality was so warped it didn't exist—she was coming with me for the love story, the happy ever after that never ever comes. As much as I want to be with her again, it is not how this is going to work, she needs to find herself in there. I see her watching me each day, waiting for me to touch her, kiss her, come to her, but I don't. I go to work and I come home, I sleep in the other room and I let her be. She walks a lot, Jameson the betrayer follows her everywhere, sleeps next to her bed at night and sits with her on the couch where she loses herself in books. I don't want her to lose herself. I need her to find herself, she will come to me when she is ready to let go of the control. My new patient is a crabby old bitch. I'm almost in a hurry for her to be done with life because her bitter negativity is sucking my soul dry. Today she was particularly bitchy so I drugged her and came back to our little stone house on the hillside, it's like a page from a picture book here. The winter colours and the golden sunlight that sets them alight as I walk back up the hill, the small house is surrounded by a wall of trees keeping it hidden.

When I get inside, Avery is still out walking Jameson, so I make a cup of coffee and stand in the little kitchen contemplating her and how she's changing. She's becoming the young twenty-something woman she should be, but beneath it all she is still a killer. Her soul bleeds because she wants this but cannot let go of that, and I have no doubt that she will still need the murderer but she desperately needs to find the person too.

When they burst through the door she is something to behold, beautiful windswept and alive. I know she's starting to feel things and that means she's going to want to feel them with me. This is why I waited. This kiss. This touch, this wall that she is climbing over to get to me. Now we can set the rules and tame the uncontrollable girl that lives inside her. Starting now she has rules, my rules.

"I waited for you to be ready to come to me, you were not ready for what I have to give you. I need to be the one in charge, Avery and you need to let me be." Her eyes mist over and she cries against my chest. I want so desperately for her to be the one I save out here. "You don't know how to follow rules or take instructions, you make your own and that is an awful responsibility to have on your shoulders, you have to let some of it go."

If I'm not in control of the people in my life I cannot keep them safe, I cannot save them. *Just like the one I wished I had saved more than any other.* We all have secrets and secretly, I want her to stop the insanity, give up, follow the rules and live. I feel more than I should for this deadly woman, and I have to keep that secret or it will get me killed.

HARMON

The darkest night is ignorance.

THE FIRST VULTURE HAS landed on the carcass of my brother's death. A strange Italian man spitting nonsense about avenging his brother and stolen fortunes. My mind is not on his ranting broken English because it is on the pictures of her that I just slid into my drawer before he came in. I'm filled with a jealous fire like no other at the fact she has left me here with this fucking responsibility to run off with a man who has no place in her life. The man drones on and then he says it.

"The little whore, he gave his fortune to her. It took me too long to find it, but he gave it to his wife's child. He never could never let go of Ellia even after he killed her." Bitter resentment pours from him as he huffs on about it. I'm pretty sure Callum killed his brother but I paid little attention to my brother back then, it was only later that I started watching very carefully.

"I'm still convinced her father murdered my brother, when I find him, he's going to pay. Then I'm coming for this company, boy. I want my brother's fortune and it's here somewhere, I know it now." He's going to be a pain in my ass I just know it, but he might just have what I need to bring her home. It had never crossed my mind to be honest but Rowan is her father and she would come home for him, or his funeral.

"I can send you right to Rowan if you like. He is of no consequence in my life."

He really isn't other than it might bring her home where I can get to her, it won't be hard once she is here, guilt is a magical thing when used properly.

The man's eyes light up and he looks at me in disbelief as I jot down the name of the wine estate. "You know he's there?" he looks confused.

"This man has hidden in plain sight for years, he never leaves the estate anymore. He is old and tired. Don't underestimate him though." I can see the change in him as he realises how close he is to getting what he has obviously been searching a long time for.

"He is an assassin, no?" The man questions.

"Was an assassin, it seems his daughter is the killer now and he makes average quality wine and wallows in it and his heartache." My mind is buzzing, this will surely bring her running home. I let it slip very quietly to my half-sister Amya where she was and that she didn't want to be found. My sister seems to have decided to return to fairest cape now that Callum is gone. Not that I care, I never met her before his funeral and I am not going to let her get what's mine. No, fuck it, things need to start moving forward now. I have given Avery more than enough time, four months is long enough to run from your responsibilities now my *lost girl* needs to come home where she belongs.

Three days later her father had a bullet between his eyes. It was almost too perfect—the assassin assassinated in his home. The clock is ticking down to the minute she comes racing back here, I can already see her sitting in that sad little graveyard mourning. Her place is here with the broken and the damned. With me. In my bed and my future. It is *my* fucking time now.

SHE RETURNED, JUST AS I knew she would, but with him by her side and she cried this time. Broken shattered sobs as her father was laid beside her mother. I watch her cling to the man beside her as she cries, that twinge of jealousy rises within me. I should be holding her. He kisses her on the cheek and wipes her tears away. She never cried for Callum, not a single tear. I know because neither did I. I don't feel what others do when someone dies. My whole family died when I was just a boy and that many deaths changes how you feel things, it switches it off. I thought she was like me, but the person kneeling on the ground falling to pieces is nothing like me at all. Amya and Robin are here again, my sister weeps for her friend and her husband holds her close. These people put great effort into pretending they are normal. I was never normal, my school councillor said I lacked empathy, I don't lack it, I just don't need it. This time there is no food or wine after, there are four bottles of whiskey and glasses on a table and there is silence. No one talks or laughs or reminisces about Rowan, I didn't know the man, but I do know that they have no idea how to feel about his death.

Avery slams a glass down on the glass table top and the noise startles everyone. "Well he's with my mother now so the fucking sadness that has consumed this place my whole life can finally end. He's with his love at last," she says with a shaky voice as her hand squeezes his. Amya wipes a tear away before she slams her glass down.

"He loved you, Avery and he never knew what to do with that. He's with his love now." I'm confused by the sentimentality of it all to be honest the man was devoid of emotion in my dealings with him. Robin follows suit, with glass slamming and memories.

"I knew every inch of his body and heart. He's with his love now." God what the hell? They make it sound like some insane Romeo and Juliet tale of being together after they are dead and gone. Who was this woman, even the vulture was on about this woman and her haunting his brother from her grave, did she have a magical pussy or something? This infernal need to be attached to someone forever defies my logical brain. His grave stone puzzled the shit out of me too, his name was bold on the top and just a number was etched below it three ones and the words. Sometimes we have to die to live. The more time I spend in their company, the more delusional it all seems to me. I see her get up and go to the kitchen and he stays, deep in conversation with Amya and I take the opportunity to go and get something else to drink. She's leaning against the counter with her eyes closed just breathing in and out the corporate diva lost and in her place a girl in black jeans and sneakers. My formidable opponent is fucked.

"Hey," I say softly so I don't frighten her. "Can we talk?"

"Sure, I guess we can." She swallows the tears that were right there a second ago.

"It can wait if you don't want to talk to me." Personable I remind myself. Fuck people are hard work.

"No it's okay, Harmon. What do you need?" You pregnant and back at work, but I cannot say that out loud.

"I'm going to be honest, Avery, I haven't a clue what I'm doing and I need you to come back and help me. The company needs you, I know it is what Callum and your father wanted for you." Play the guilt card.

"My father and Callum may have wanted it but they never gave a shit what I wanted Harmon. I'm staying, Mat and I will stay on the estate and I will help you where I can, but I'm not going back to that life." Oh but you are little lost girl.

"Please think about it, Avery. It would have hurt Callum so much to see it all falling apart." I try to get her to feel that emotional connection, she needs to feel guilty for letting him down. He had high hopes for her and I'm going to make her think she has failed.

"It isn't hard, Harmon, most of it runs itself." She counters me again.

"Please, just a few hours a week until I know what's going on?" I try to sound desperate, I know what's going on in fact I have things under control. Sneaky Sam has been a busy boy.

"I'll ask Mat," she says before leaving the kitchen and going back to them. *Ask Mat?* What has happened to her? What has he done? I stay inside for a long time to try and calm the anger and irritation, I need this to be easy not hard. Mat has got to go. She has nothing to lose if I fail, but I am not going back to what I was before, this the chance I waited all my life for and I am not about to let the doctor ruin it. Him and I need to have a little talk before I leave today, he needs to get out of my way.

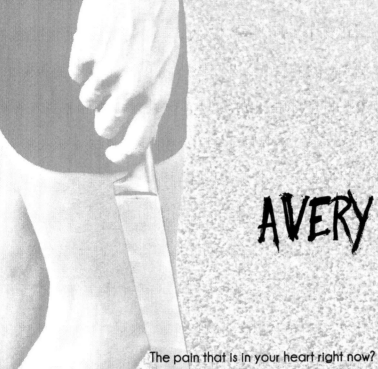

AVERY

The pain that is in your heart right now?
Imagine you can reach it by touching it in someone else with
the intent to heal it. We are all connected.

RULES, THOSE THINGS that have consequences if I didn't follow them. And for the first time in my life, I had strict boundaries and all I wanted was to rebel and break them all. The first time I got punished for breaking Mathew's rules, I wanted to run away. I felt like a scorned child. Then I realised I had never felt that—not once in my life. If I didn't like the rules, I broke them or made my own and no one ever called me out or punished me. No one had loved me enough to stop me from destroying myself. As long as I didn't feel anything, they were happy to let me raise hell. But with Mat, at first it was horrific. I broke the rules a thousand times before I learned that his harshness was out of love. At first, he was so hard on me, but as I slowly learned to follow the rules, things changed and his punishment became guidance. I thought about my actions and their consequences something I had never done, I never took a minute to think about what my actions did to others. I was a selfish little bitch.

That first time, Mathew took me over his knee and smacked my backside till it burned. I cried, I broke, I hated him and I loved him and everything between. When he was done and my skin burned like fire he put me on the bed and made love to me, not soft love. He fucked me so I could feel the punishment, my ass in the air and my hands in his death grip behind my back. Not the worst punishment I suffered, but this was the day the dam wall broke and I stopped being that girl and worked very single minute on being this woman. He had to break me to heal me, he explained it after, after I was better. Now punishments are few and far between and mostly they end in rough sex and both of us feeling satisfied and loved. Mathew tries to tell me that this is just a season he isn't my forever that he is just here to show me how to live and love. The rules were simple, yet I still failed often. My own stubborn nature and the fact I never had to follow rules before saw me punished often. Simple rules, keep our small home tidy. Be waiting for him when he got home, clean showered and well groomed. Walk the dog, learn to cook—that one I've earned a free pass on because I just cannot get it right. Go to bed with him every night, not before him, not after him, with him.

I got lost in a book one night, sucked away to another world, I didn't notice him get up and go to bed. I felt sick, the fear of being punished made it hard to swallow as I put the book away. My hands trembled and my knees felt weak as I padded down the small passage to our room. Too afraid to stop and pee, I crept quietly into the room, the darkness here is not like the city, it is pitch black. I could feel my heart racing and I hoped he couldn't hear it, and that I didn't wake him. I would still be punished in the morning, which would be worse because I would never sleep. my breath catches in my dry throat as he flicks on the light next to the bed and walks towards me. He's naked except for his boxer shorts and even in my fear, I appreciate the man I get to see. He sits down on the end of the bed his angry eyes burn holes in my fragile heart. I lurch forward to put my arms around him and apologise, but he shoves me away before I get close. Stumbling over my own feet, I fall down and land between his. My tears fall on the floor and I know he's disappointed in me. He lifts me up by my ponytail, my stinging scalp makes me cry more.

"When do you go to bed, Avery?" He asks me, calm but angry at my disregard for his rules.

"When you do." I answer sniffing away my tears, if I don't answer this will be ten times worse.

"Come, angel, let me take you to bed." He tugs my hair so have to follow him. But it's not our soft warm bed he takes me to. No, I spend the night in the small hall closet, too tiny to sit down so I have to stand all night. Alone in the pitch black darkness, I'm sure this is how a coffin must feel inside. The claustrophobic space made me cry, scream and beg as terror controlled me. Anger poured out with every curse. How dare he lock me away! I have handled having my ass smacked raw or standing in a corner for hours not allowed to even look around. Humiliated and treated like the child I never got to be, but this was too much. It was too much because I was alone and not with him. I didn't fall in love fast, or at first sight. I feel in love alone in a dark closet. As he had broken me down to nothing and let me rebuild myself better, I had slowly fallen in love with him. I had not even realised it while it happened, but alone in that dark closet I learned my lesson and I learned what love is. I loved him, even if he didn't love me back and that terrified me.

A few weeks ago I got a letter by courier from Amya, I have no idea how she found me, but she hasn't told the rest of them where I was. She just wanted me to know that they worry. It made me feel terrible, I hid the letter from Mathew and tried to push it out of my mind. I saved her number to my new phone and texted her one message.

I am fine please leave me alone. I am happy here.

She didn't reply and I think she just wanted me to know that somewhere they knew I was gone. I was happy to be gone.

I was cooking when the world ended for me again. Jameson was hovering under my feet in the desperate hopes that I would drop something and he could eat it. My phone chimed on the counter, I thought it was Mat, the old lady is on her last days and he said she has given him a date for her suicide. I hope it was him with a sexy message telling me to wait in the room, or to be ready for a good spanking. I loved the surrender that I was able to give him when we had sex, I had always controlled my sex life it was never about passion it was about the kill after. Now it is raw passion, feelings that come alive as actions. I wipe my hands on my apron and touch the screen to see what it is he has planned for tonight, one message wrecked me. In one second I was ruined.

Avery, I know u r are happy but ur father has been killed. My heart won't let me bury him without u here. Please come home.

I felt myself cracking and the pieces are falling to the floor around me where I end up in a puddle of my own tears. Jameson sits next to me resting his head on me, it's like he just knows the heartache is unbearable. The sun has set and the air is cold even though it is spring already the nights get icy here. I'm still stuck on the floor in the kitchen when I hear the front door, fear seizes me, I have broken all the rules and I scramble to stand. When I do I see his face go from angry disappointment to care and concern.

"Avery?" He approaches me with caution, I wonder some days if he still thinks I might kill him. When he gets closer I collapse on the floor again. "Avery what's wrong?" He sits down next to me. "I'm not angry, I won't punish you. Just tell me what happened?" He's holding me. I hand him my phone because I don't think I can say the words out loud yet. I have lost people before this, I was born into loss, but never have I felt it. The deep agonising pain of knowing my father is gone, is made worse by that the last words we spoke were in anger. That hurts the most, I know that my words were like daggers to him and I can't take them back I can't even say sorry. Mat holds me as I sit on the cold floor and the pieces he has worked so hard to put back together just fall apart. I was a shitty daughter and I will never get the chance to right that wrong. I feel this in the deepest parts of me, but it aches a little less because he holds me tight and tells me it will all be okay. And I believe it will be.

We stay there for ages, I feel stiff and weak when he carries me to bed and kisses my forehead.

"I'm going to go take care of the old lady, then tomorrow I will take you home, baby. I will be there. I'm not just going to leave you, if you still need me, I will be with you." *If? Is he serious? Of course I need him, there is no if, I need him more than ever.* I sniff away my tears and wipe my face with my hands.

"Thank you." I muster the two little words that cannot even express the gratitude in my heart, because I know that had I not been here this would have ended me. It might still.

When he came back late that night I could tell his heart was as heavy as mine, something was weighing on him too. As he held me close, I felt the sinking feeling that today was the beginning of the end of us, I don't want to let him go. I try to show him, I turn and kiss him. He kisses me back and it feels like goodbye, so I kiss him harder. His hands tangle in my knotted hair as he pulls me onto him, the fire is there like it has been since the very beginning only it is just smouldering tonight. I pull at his shirt, trying to get at the skin below, to get to him to cling on with everything I have. Straddling him, I pull my dress up over my head, my tattoos and breasts right in front of him. The dark glint is back in his eyes as his hands pull me back to him by my nipples, the sharp pain makes me squeeze my thighs against him and I can feel the buckle of his belt rub against my lace knickers. He shoves me off him and onto my back, he kneels between my thighs towering over me, the grin I want to see is missing from his face as he pulls my underwear to the side and slides a finger inside me. My body bows to let him go deeper, I crave the way he makes me feel. His fingers continue as he bends over me and kisses my skin. His kisses never land on the coloured side, the clean slate the empty side where the pale whiteness I inherited from my mother glows in the dull light. His lips are warm against my cool, exposed body and the slightest lick of his tongue drives me closer to the edge. I need this so much, I need him. I try so hard to follow his rules, I let him touch me and make me feel, but my hands can't stay away tonight and I slide them over his shoulders digging my fingernails into his flawless skin. I feel the growl of disapproval on my skin as he bites me. His fingers are gone in a second, making me gasp loudly as he pulls himself away from me and back onto his knees. I lift up onto my elbows so I can see him unbuckle the belt and pop the top button of his jeans, I catch myself biting my lips and wanting to touch myself.

"Roll over, Avery, hands under the pillow." There he is. I do as I am told although I wouldn't mind having my ass smacked. I sense it isn't what he needs. My knees are pushed up underneath me so my ass is up in the air, I turn my head to the side so I can see him in the mirror on the wall beside us, he slides off the bottom of the bed and steps out of his pants. I can only see his shadow from this angle, a shadow that shows me his hard cock and masculine shape perfectly. The dark outline on the wall reflected in the mirror as he stalks back onto the bed. Smack. His hand lands across my thighs that I have squeezed together in antici-pation and the desperate need for relief. The tearing sound as my underwear is ripped at the side seams is amplified by the look on his face as he does it with malice. Mathew's angry and hurting and I want to fix it, *this is fixing it. Let him use your body to feel what he needs to feel.* There is a distinct difference between feeling sex and watching it, as I watch him bury his face in my cunt, my body reacts but my mind is on the image I see. His tongue tortures me in the best way possible, fingers digging into the flesh of my hips as he holds them still so I can't control the pressure. Mathew is in control. Our breathing is the only sound in the room. Heavy breaths hissing in and out. I suffocate my moans by biting my upper arm. I can see his hand wrapped around his cock as he strokes himself to the same rhythm of his tongue the visual makes my back arch and his grip tighten on my thigh, where I'm sure his fingers will leave marks. The skin has gone white around his fingers. I see it in the reflection of us as he lets go and I lose the feeling of his mouth against me. A whimper escapes as he drapes over my whole body, I feel his cock as it rests against my ass. "I'm not done yet," he whispers over my back and I sigh in both desire and relief. "Stay still, Avery." An instruction, a rule to follow. My body tenses to keep from moving and I feel the thudding in my chest, I'm waiting to fail and feel the punishment. I can never stay still. His hand slides down the side of my body, I watch it travel from my breast to my ass and he shifts to fit it between us. He touches me and I want to move but I try not to. "Still." He reminds me. His fingers move the wetness from earlier up to my ass. He knows that is a no, the one thing I won't do. *He knows.* My muscles are so tight they begin to ache and fear makes me shake, I cannot stop it. I want to yell out at him to stop, but I can see his face in the mirror and I know he won't listen even if I do. "Please." I let out one soft whimper as his finger slides in causing pain to ricochet through me. "Still, I need this. I need to take this from you, Avery. I need to cancel him out before we go back there." *He knows that Eiran hurt me, and that the fear of that agony rules me.* "Avery, I'm going to fuck your ass tonight, how much it hurts is on you." He wants to hurt me, I try to tell myself it is to fix me but this isn't about me tonight. My grief and pain is forgotten in his need to know I would give up myself for him. I stop watching. I close my eyes and let silent tears snake out as I feel him moving his finger inside, the pain I fear is there but I wanes with each stroke. Mathew has told me about self-sacrifice and giving yourself over to helping other person is the thing that makes us human and I know that is what he is trying to tell me now. *Put him first, give him your pain because he needs it. I have learned to be human it doesn't take away the fear of my past though.* Amazingly as I accept this and surrender the pain is forgotten—all of it. The pain of my father dying, the pain of losing Callum, the agony of killing Eiran and I don't even feel my skin tear as he pushes into me. I don't feel the blood curdling scream leaving my lungs. In my pain. I'm human. "Finally . . . my angel, you feel," Mathew says as he rocks inside me, my eyes are open and I watch now. The furious movements of his body against mine, the way he is holding onto me keeping me still, taking what he needs not giving me what I need. The scars of my youth are finally healed, Mathew is sad because he fixed me. I know he's getting ready to be done with me. It smothers my happiness and I feel like I am waiting for the world to end as we both orgasm. My body quakes below his as he comes inside my ass. The one place I asked him not to touch. The thing I gave to him anyway.

"Why did you need to fix me?" the words come out with my tears. *Why? This hurts me. Everything fucking hurts now.*

"Because I couldn't save someone once. Now I need to save as many as I can to make it right."

I feel his pain with my own as he cleans me, the warm cloth stings where he wipes me. I let a hiss out. He kisses me softly on the back and pulls me to lie against him. "I don't want you to leave me." The begging in my soul can be heard in my voice. "Not yet, angel. Go to sleep. I'm taking you home soon."

NOT MATTHEW

If you truly loved yourself you could never hurt another.

THIRTEEN HOURS IN a car is long even when you're not sad. Avery is sad so the drive is painful, her father is dead and she carries guilt and grief over it. But more than that she's afraid. With every kilometre drawing us closer to home, her fear consumes more of her, she's reverting to the girl who was so afraid to feel that she was hollow inside. It is too soon for her to go back, she only just set herself free. My time with her is almost up, I saved her from the end I knew she was going to find and set her on a new path. Now I have to let her go without hurting her too much. With every goodbye in life, we learn something, I have said many goodbyes—they always follow a hello. I knew that I would have to set her free or give her peace. When we are almost halfway through our journey she asks me quietly. "Who was the one you didn't save?" Those two violently beautiful eyes look right inside me.

"My sister." No one has asked me before, no one ever bothered to know my why.

"What happened?" She holds my hand over the gap between the seats.

"She had cancer . . . leukemia." I look at the road and remember her bald head and sad eyes. "She begged me to kill her, she couldn't take the pain any longer. I couldn't do it. I let her suffer until she did it herself." I let her down and I will never stop trying to make that feeling go away.

"I understand it now." Avery looks away out the side window and I believe she really does. We stop at every single service station so Jameson can pee, I have come to accept he isn't mine any longer. He is her dog, the traitor.

The wine estate she calls home comes into view in the early hours of the following morning, the birds are awake but the sky is still dark. She gets out and punches in a security code to open the giant iron gates that keep the world out. Instead of getting back in the car, she starts to walk up the gravel driveway and I follow slowly in the car, the headlights lighting her way. The big white gabled home is situated at the end of it, Avery uses keys that she has been swinging between her fingers for hours now to open the gate and door. I wait a minute, not sure yet if I'm welcomed to join her, when she turns around and looks at me, waiting. I get out and we enter the house together. Jameson is at her heels right away. The eerie silence of this whole place makes me feel like I'm trespassing on her life. She flips on lights as we go, the long passage ends in an open lounge and kitchen. Avery goes straight to the kitchen, fills the kettle and turns it on. She's learned not to drink alcohol as a crutch so coffee is her go-to drink when she needs comfort now. I sit on a bar stool at the island leaving the space she has created between us. When the sun rises in a few hours, it will be the day of her father's funeral and I know that she will need me close then, now she needs space. After coffee and retrieving our bags from the car we sleep for a few hours tangled in each other on the couch, there are beds but she didn't seem to want to sleep in any of the rooms.

The heat of the sun baking us through the windows is what wakes me. I'm covered in sweat and stuck to the couch. My shirt is soaked where Avery has draped herself over me. Her dark hair is spread over her face, I push it aside so I can see her, I'm sure only a few people have had the pleasure of waking up with her. Seeing her, exposed vulnerable and absolutely beautiful. Being back here though I don't know how long I can stay, Callum told me his plan before he died—it's a stupid one. I cannot imagine anything worse for the woman who has come alive with me over the past few months than being trapped in their world that way, I know Harmon won't let it be. He's going to try which means I'm in his way. I never planned on staying in her life and I still don't, I just don't want to hurt her beyond repair when I go. She is still fragile in her humanity and a small thing could shatter it all.

My fingers run through her hair, silky strands of almost black, the knots from the car and sleep snag in my fingers. I'm so hot lying here, I secretly want her to wake. I start being an ass by tickling her ear and her cheek with a piece of her hair,

I have got to move it's sweltering. At the very least, a window needs to be opened. She swats at my hand and starts to roll over a little, she opens just her blue eye and gives me the look. "You ass," she mutters half asleep through a yawn.

"Morning, beautiful. Can I get up and open a window please, I'm dying in here." I ask her nicely.

"Ugh. I'm sweated to you. All stuck, gross yes get up go and open a window." She's mortified as she shoves herself up freeing me and revealing a nice big sweaty patch on my shirt. Sometimes there's nothing romantic about sleeping together, sometimes it's just gross. I swing my legs over and stand up to get some air in here, opening the big sliding door to the patio outside. I take a step out into the late morning, the sun is hot and there is not a breath of wind. The vines don't move, they're stagnant in the humid heat of the valley. Pulling my sweaty shirt over my head and leaving it on the table, I go stand at the railing and let the sun shine on my skin. It's there, I have to remind myself that this day is going to get sad in just a few hours. I look over my shoulder and Avery is walking towards me with coffee and a sorrowful smile on her face. I thought we had an hour or two. We stand in silence while we drink our coffee and sunshine in, this place is magnificent. I didn't appreciate its beauty when I sneaked in before. This place is the foundation of her life, where she began and where she was destroyed.

"I'm going to shower and get changed." She looks at me, and my heart is torn because I have one more thing she needs to face and it needs to be now.

"No. I'll come we can have a *bath*." Her face falls and I see the fear choking her already, she has not once since she came with me got in a bath, she has told me why and now it's time to fix it. The last piece of the toxic love that crippled her is going to be removed and it will be today, now before we bury her past. I grab her hand in mine, her palm is sweaty and she's shaking but trying very hard to hide it. I lead her down the passage to what I am sure was her father's master suite, she freezes at the door and I have to yank her inside. His bed is stripped to the mattress and a blood stain is still visible on the exposed fabric. "Mathew, I can't do this, let's just go back to the mountain." Oh sweet Avery. I cannot ever go back where I have been, that's not how it works for an angel of death. "No, Avery, don't make me angry. We're doing this right now." I'm firm with her, she needs this. She submits and follows me through the room to the master bath, a big stone bath sits in the very center of the room. Her fear comes to life, her monsters need to be exorcised and this tub is where we are going to do it. I'm going to make her forget why she hates a bath and make her remember it for only one thing—me. I turn on the water to fill it up and swing around to where she stands tears glisten at the corner of her eyes but she won't let them fall. Her breaths are ragged and her fears are manifesting into panic as I stand right in front of her. Lifting her chin so she can look at me, I slowly start to undress her, each button exposes her, makes her vulnerable and even more attractive. Her body is a human contradiction, the one half dark art and images cover every bit of her and the other is the pure milky white unspoilt skin. I kiss along the line that divides her into who she is and what she is, we all have a line hers is just drawn on for me to see. I'm two very different halves sewn together with a delicate thread that seamlessly joins what I am and who I am into the quiet blessing of a peaceful end to those who desire it. Everyone has two faces, just look in the mirror you will see. "Get in the water, Angel." I kiss her softly, giving her an instruction. Her eyes beg me to say she doesn't have to, but I won't. "Get in, Avery." I leave the tap to run as she does what she is told, she doesn't sit down just stands there in the water with her eyes down and her hands ball into fists. I remove my pants and step in with her. The water is a little too hot but I sit anyway, the burn as it turns my skin red is a reminder to me of how much this will hurt her. She's shivering where she stands towering above me. "Come sit." I move my legs so there is space for her between them. She turns around and sits with her back to me, curled over hugging her knees to her chest rocking back and forth. Pulling her towards me, the water makes little waves that flow back and forth for a while before they settle. I hold her as her fears seize the heart she has just learned to follow. I wait. I give her time before I take what I need and replace that fear, replace Eiran and drown the last of her torment. When I feel her body soften and the worst of her fears have left her, I know she is ready for me. Turning her around to face me, I look in her eyes. I see her defeat and now it's time to change it back to fight. I kiss her as I slowly snake my hands around her delicate neck. It's time she learned that rules are not meant to be followed blindly that the voice in her should still guide her. In a swift move, I force her away from me and under the water, her arms flail and nails scratch and rip at the skin on my arms her eyes are wide begging me from beneath the water to let her up for air. *Not yet.* I wait to see if she stops fighting, but she doesn't. Her legs are now kicking out at me. There it is. All of her in one place at last, I let her go and she explodes out of the water still lashing out at me, I grab her wrists in my one hand and her face in the other. "Stop now, you have to know when to fight, when to follow your instinct and when to stop." She's sucking in air as she tries to stop the natural fight of being held below the water. "You can stop now, now we make this better." Her mouth is on mine in seconds, our tongues fight her fear and anger in a furious war. She grabs my cock in her hand like a vice grip making me moan into her open mouth. Fuck. Shit. Damn. She's fighting back, I can't afford to lose a fight with her, not now. I grab her hand in mine and make eye contact so she knows that I still make the rules, for now. "Turn around, put your arms over the end of the tub on the floor." I see the defiance right there in her eyes but she turns around on her knees and hangs her arms out of the bath, the water is just below the curve of her ass leaving it exposed to my hand. I smack it hard and she stiffens. "You want to defy me don't you, Avery? You want to fight me?" I smack her again for not answering.

"Yes!" Her strangled reply comes in a hissing sound as I smack her again. "Fuck yes."

"Why don't you, little angel?" I rub the red flesh softly and kneel close behind her. "Why don't you fight me?" I slide two fingers inside her and she bows her spine to let me, her thighs moving apart.

"Because I don't *need* to fight you." She learns so fast.

"That's right, but sometimes you are going to have to fight." I kiss up her spine and continue to fuck her with my fingers. I lift her so she is standing in the bath and her hands are flat on the floor outside it. Exposed, open and all mine, bending her so her belly rests on the stone side, she's contorted into a position where she cannot move and I slide my cock inside her. It feels like heaven, she tenses as I push hard, her body slammed against the side. Water cascading onto the floor around her, I fuck her lithe body hard enough to leave bruises. Her pussy squeezes me hard as the pain brings her close to her release and all I want is to take this feeling with me forever, the feeling of her body becoming mine. I have to pull out because in my haste, I didn't bring a condom to the bath, and Avery doesn't need a baby, not mine and not Harmon's. *I need to sort that quickly.* The thought enters my head, I need to protect her before I leave. The scream as she comes on my cock could shatter the mirrors on the walls, I pull out in time to come on the hand print I left on her ass. She is mine, but only for now. I lift her back into the water and turn the tap on to warm it up. We lie in there for a short while just breathing, just understanding.

"Thank you," she whispers after a while, I know I have done everything I set out to do and now I need to start setting her free. She has been saved from herself.

AFTER THE FUNERAL, we drink. She drinks the most I have seen in months, she clings to me as she lets the past go and realizes that her future is here now. The limbo is over. I see Harmon, watching us all day, I notice he doesn't cry or even look sad. Harmon looks confused at the outpouring of love and emotion, the man is a hollow shell of humanity and she's going to have to fight him on her own. *Don't trust him my little angel. It is not my job to tell her the things I know, but I will make sure she can fight fair.* I had planned for this, I knew what he wanted from her and I came ready. After they all leave and she collapses on the bed in her childhood room, I get my bag and search out the vile I brought with me. I inject the sleeping queen with contraceptive. At least I know she is safe for four months, I will ask Owen to step in and help me when it wears off, because I'll be long gone. The following day is spent wandering around the estate with her telling me about it, the boarded up restaurant that was her mother's. Twenty-five years later, it's falling apart and looks like a scene from a bad thriller, she sits on the little deck swinging her legs over the edge. Her sadness follows us all day, I'm glad she's feeling this, it shows me she can actually deal with life now. "This is the spot where my Mom told Rowan she was pregnant, this place was her dreams come true." The absence of her mother in her life was a huge part of the imbalance in her personality. Rowan never got over the heartache of her death and in turn couldn't be free to love his child. Callum would share stories with me over the time I treated him and especially after he decided he was not going to fight any longer. I feel like I had a window into their lives through his eyes, I know just how isolated she was. She spends a lot of the day in silent reflection. I just stay close to her because that's all she needs today. "Harmon asked me to go back to work." She says as we walk down the gravel path to the graveyard. "And, do you want to go back to work?" She has to make her own choices now, I can guide her but she has to decide her path forward.

"I should, but I don't know what I want anymore." She reaches for my hand and the connection is warm and it feels right, us here, in this place together. "Callum always wanted me to be the one, then I read his letter and I felt like I have no choice. Add that to my mother's letters telling me to choose my path and find what makes my heart sing and I think maybe I wasn't meant to be like them." She's thinking with more than just her head at last, she's considering her feelings and what she needs. I have no doubt that she will return to their world—who am I kidding—our world at some point. I just want her to do it on her terms and with a heart that isn't made of stone.

We end our day on the patio with her mother's wine and a simple dinner. I know I have to go, yet I'm clinging to the idea of staying just a little longer, I keep saying just a bit more. It's wrong and it is giving her false hope in the love she has for me. Don't get me wrong, I love all my patients and I have always seen her as that, a patient, a case. I love her deeply, but I never have been or will be in love with her. *I was sent her for a reason and a season and both have passed, I have another job waiting for me far from here.*

AVERY

Mostly it is loss that teaches us about the worth of things.

WHEN YOU FEEL something for the first time, it's amplified. The feelings are bigger and stronger that time than any time after that. Your first love, sadness, pain, your first real loss. My first loss was not just one thing, the magnified agony that was my first loss encompassed so much more. I lost my father, I lost Callum, I lost my mother, I lost Eiran and I lost Mathew all at once and I felt it down to my bones. I woke up three days after my father's funeral with Jameson lying next to me and Not Mathew. I thought he got up to make coffee or go for a run, but if he was running, Jameson would have gone with him. Clambering out of bed I try and find something to put on my naked body, the aches of last nights sex reminding me I'm a human. The lazy dog doesn't even move as I slip on an over-sized T-shirt and walk out of my room. The house is still closed up and dark and I can't smell coffee or hear Mathew. I know it before I really know it, Mathew has gone, the season and reason have passed and he has left me. I always knew he wasn't my forever, he told me that, but secretly I wished he could be.

The days that passed after he left seemed to go by in slow motion, dragging me down into the pits of despair and holding my head below water so that I was drowning in my own heartache. He didn't just leave and say nothing, no, Mathew, or Not Mathew was a good man and he left me a letter.

Avery

My beautiful little angel, I'm not abandoning or leaving you, please don't be hurt by my departure. The time has come for you to live and I mean really truly live your life, whatever that life is meant to be. You are strong and you know the true power of your own heart, you know how and when to fight if you need to. Follow that feeling that is in you. Be human, be selfless and never be afraid to feel the consequences of your actions. As long as we are together, we will suffer and you deserve so much more than the suffering that being attached to me would cause. I know that being a killer is in your blood as being a healer is in mine, just remember that what you do affects others as well as you.

Colours fade, even black and white fade into shadows but they can still be seen, you have left a permanent shadow in my world.

I want you to do one thing for me, please with all my heart I ask that you go and read Callum's will. It's important, Avery. Be wary of Harmon and guard that fragile heart, it only just learned to beat.

Jameson is yours, he stopped being mine the day you got into my car, the dog loves you and you him. Keep him. Love him. Remember me when you are with him, because I'm never not with you. If you ever feel alone and that you need someone to talk to my friend Owen knows I have left and he will always be there, his number is saved in your phone. He's a notorious dick as a boyfriend so don't go there, but he is good man and friend that can be trusted. Please don't kill him, I like him.

Our season and reason have passed, but let our lessons not be forgotten. I love you enough to let you go.

Yours

My name was never Mathew

Xxx

I returned to work a week later with one thing in mind, I wanted to know what Harmon had to do to keep his half and how I could give him mine. I don't want any part of the family business any longer. I'm going to make wine and walk my dog. The circumstances of my father's death still haunt me, how did Baldini find him and how long before they come for me? I, after all have the Baldini fortune, O'Reilly technically bought their companies when I was six and the money was put into a trust for me until my recent running away, I'd never touched it, nor do I care to do it again. That money is stained in my mother's blood and I want nothing to do with it.

It is so easy to slip back into old ways, I slipped right back in where I left off as if nothing had changed at all. I had some things I wanted to change though, getting them past Harmon who seems to be enjoying his new found power has been tricky. He is like a clone of Callum just younger, driven and hungry for power and control. I sit at my desk tapping my nails and reading shipping reports when the door opens and Sam bursts in. "You're back." I roll my eyes at his enthusiasm, he really is painful, that hasn't changed at all. "Hi, Sam." I don't look up from my screen.

"Would you like to join Sam and I for lunch, Avery?" I glare up at Harmon standing over me and my desk.

"No, not really. That vegan shit does nothing for me thanks." I snarl, since when does Sam 'do lunch' unless Harmon is gay, but given the way he looks at my ass that's not the team he plays for.

"Avery, come for lunch. I don't eat that shit either. He can get a fucking salad wherever we go." I don't want, but I don't need to fight now. So I just go.

"Fine. I'll follow you. I'm not driving in Sam's car." I stand up and grab the keys for my Dad's car out of my drawer.

"Neither am I, you can ride with me," Harmon says and I know that tone, he is telling me not asking me. *Fight.*

"No thank you I can drive myself, where are we going?"

"Waterfront," Sam chimes in from near the door.

"Fine let's go." The fresh air out of the office might do me good and clear the filthy mood that is brewing. I take the stairs to avoid being stuck in the lift with the two of them. I think I'm secretly jealous that Sam and Harmon are friends, if you can call them that. The heavy door into the garages squeaks as I push it open, they are both waiting there for me, fuck it. "Can I drive with you?" Sam asks this time, NO. "Sure Sam." I push the button to unlock the car and ignore Harmon. I can't be asked to have them both in a car with me. I lift myself into the big SUV and start it. I see Harmon shaking his head as he gets into his Mercedes. God, he's just like Callum, they even like the same cars.

Lunch was painful, all they talked about was work. I wanted to get up and leave before we even got our drinks. After our mediocre meal, Harmon looks at me I see a smirk on his face as he asks.

"How's Mathew doing?" I want to burst into tears and leave, but I don't.

"Mathew is gone, Harmon, but I'm sure the idiots you have following me, told you that already." I had a good shadow for years and I knew he was there, Harmon's goons were so easy to spot. His and the Italians, though I'm pretty sure they are just following to keep tabs now that Callum isn't here they don't trust women in power. Sam looks confused at the standoff happening in front of him. I have been watching him too, only my shadows are a little better versed at keeping themselves out of sight.

"I don't know what you think they are going to see or tell you, but they are not very good. Also, there is nothing to see." He sips on his drink and stares at me with a look of shock on his face as if he cannot possibly believe I have caught him out.

"Who's Mathew?" Sam the annoyance chimes in again.

"His name is not Mathew and he saved me Sam. That's all you, or anyone needs to know." I glare at him the threat doesn't need to be spoken Sam has known me for years.

"So when he locked you in a cupboard for two days that was saving you?" Harmon digs his claws into an open wound. *Fight.*

"You should try it sometime, life would be so peaceful with you in a closet. I'd throw the fucking key away." He doesn't know what I am capable of and he should stop.

"Avery, you let a man lock you in a closet?" Sam again. I feel attacked.

"Sam, fuck off." I snap grabbing my keys and getting up. This was a shitty lunch.

"But I came with you," he yells after me as I storm off and I flip him the bird over my shoulder. No one will ever understand what Mathew did for me least of all those two idiots.

HARMON

The darkest night is ignorance.

AVERY PASSES IN AND out of the office as she pleases, no one has the balls to call her out and I'm desperately trying to be the nice guy. I have less than eighteen months to get her in line and make this work. I need to change my tactics and woo her or something, but nothing seems to interest her except the farm and the doctor's dog. I have the fucking Italians breathing down my neck. Every move I make, they counter and we are losing business all over the place. Things are not going to plan and it is driving me crazy, this was supposed to be easy. Getting woman into bed is not hard, I look like their walking wet dreams. Yet Avery treats me like I have the bubonic plague, I think she is angry that Callum left half the business to me. What the hell is wrong with her?

"You have an invite to an event with the president, addressed to yourself and Avery. You have six calls from Baldini and one from Sam." The airhead that answers my phones chatters on next to me going over schedules, meetings, messages and shit I have no interest in at all. But that invitation catches my eye, Avery would have to spend the night with me being civil, this could be exactly what we need. I look at it the gold embossed letters and expensive stationary reek of government overspending, this idiot has now been in power so long it's sick, he became the Robert Mugabe of South Africa by changing laws so no one could vote him out in the most dictated democracy ever. Where do I benefit? He's corrupt and easy to manipulate. He wants something from me, if we are getting an invite, there is always something they *need*. I am going to step up my plan and this is my chance to get what I need a little more directly.

My mind cannot focus on anything and I feel the urge to travel biting but I don't want to let her out of my sights for too long I need a distraction because focusing on only one thing is giving me blue balls and a headache.

"What do you want to do first, sir?" She's still there.

"You," I growl.

"Took you long enough to ask, your brother couldn't even get it up and he tried." She bats her fake lashes at me, I need to fuck something before I go crazy and she is here.

"Close the blinds." It's after eleven the chances of Avery showing up are nil at this point. I push my chair back and lose my belt buckle as she walks back to my desk, she is a bit thick around the middle. Her hair is blonde and mousy, not my usual taste but I will take what I can get today, maybe I will be able to focus on work after this. She stands in front of me looking like the cat that got the canary. "Lose your knickers and hike that skirt up, leave your shoes on." She follows instructions well, I guess it comes naturally when that's all you do in the day. "Get on your knees and use those fake lips to get my cock hard."

Like a good little lap dog she does as she is told, her dick sucking skills could use work but I haven't had a good fuck in months so it doesn't take much to get me ready to go. I pull her up by her hair sprayed ponytail and pull her onto my lap. She makes a move to kiss me. I grip her by the neck and speak slowly so she understands. "That whorish mouth is not going near my lips, get on and fuck me before I lose interest." She lowers herself onto my cock and I instantly feel the relief I've been craving. There's something carnal about sex, it is a need in all of us and when it is denied we become twisted and distorted. The stupid woman bounces up and down on my cock, I remind myself this is just release and try to remove myself from the slutty noises she makes and imagine the sounds Avery would make instead. I wish I could kiss her and touch her, but she is a filler, a place holder because since my brother shared his warped plan with me my mind cannot accept anyone but Avery into it. I crumple a financial report of my desk and stick it in her mouth making her eyes bulge, but the noise is distracting me. Grabbing her hips, I force her to move faster and harder, I need this to be over. Her boobs are in my face even though her top is still on, it's so revealing I can see the whole show. I focus on them and not her face. She isn't enjoying this the deer in headlights eyes give it away. "Fuck me like you want to." I hiss at her because she is not putting any effort into this. Her body moves with renewed energy and I can feel myself getting close. Shoving her hard to the floor again I pull the paper out of her mouth and she gasps a breath before I ram my cock in her dry mouth, two thrusts and come down her throat and she gags as I hold her head still with me half way down her esophagus. When I look up from her mascara stained face, I am met with another—Avery. The disgust is blatant as she shakes her head stepping over the whores undies on the floor to get to her desk.

"Don't let me stop you," she says an angry smile on her face as she sits at her desk, the idiot on her knees is frozen in terror before me and I lift her chin so she has to look at me.

"Good girl, now get the fuck out." I growl my voice low. This has set me back again, why can I not get it right with her? Why wasn't she attracted to me?

As the door closes behind the mortified girl, I greet Avery.

"Morning, I mean afternoon, Avery, it is almost afternoon, so nice of you to actually come to work today."

"Fuck off, Harmon. You're not my boss." She snaps at me. I need to be nice to her, maybe if I tried to be nicer. I cannot help the deep hatred in me though, this is the girl that has lived the life that always should have been mine. It's not fair, if I didn't need her so fucking much I would be focused on revenge, but being with me will be revenge enough. The phone buzzes and I see that Italian vultures number so I click ignore.

"We have an invitation to a government gala evening, I think we should at-tend, its important." I try sounding nice, I try so hard.

"Fine, get your fuck-toy to put it in my calendar." No resistance, no fight just yes. Maybe nice is the answer. She's distracted by something I can see it, she is focused so deeply on the screen in front of her.

"Does it, I mean she, bother you?" I cannot help myself. She stands up so she is looking right at me.

"I shared an office with Callum since I was fifteen, your brother fucked every single assistant he had at that desk and he didn't care if is I saw it or not, so no it doesn't *bother* me in the least, Harmon. I am used to it. I will say, next time, use a condom because that whore has fucked almost every manager from the first floor up, you might get something nasty." The sneer on her face tells me she is enjoying this little moment of cattiness, maybe she's a little jealous after all. She is jealous, that must be it. She is jealous because I haven't flirted with her.

"As long as we are good, we do have a company to run together." I get the death glare before she walks back out of the office.

"Fuuuuuuuuuck" I yell aloud into the empty room. I hate her.

The phone is going again, that man is relentless.

AVERY

What doesn't kill me, might make me kill you.

T HE FOUL DISPLAY of public fucking in my office churned my stomach more than I will ever admit to that man. He's invading every aspect of my life and I feel a festering hate and a need to murder someone creeping back in. I try to remember that there would be consequence I even try to find one but I can't. He's like a wart on my happiness and I need to find out what he wants from me and get rid of him. For good. He tries so hard to be nice to me, I see that underlying malice. He needs me for something and I'm not going to give him anything—ever. I have no idea what Callum was thinking bringing him here, but I don't actually care at all. I leave the office and his smug face to go and oversee a shipment of explosives and munitions that is being sent to North Africa, war is such a lucrative business. This container is the exact reason our President is buttering us up, these under the table deals are all politically fuelled and if we are on his side we are not against him. The foolish man thinks we are loyal—loyalty is for family and no one else. I am loyal to no one, but I favour those with the finance and influence to benefit me.

I can't push the dull ache of missing Mathew away, it still hurts. I miss him, I miss the rules and the loneliness cuts me deeper every single night that I lie there staring at the ceiling wishing for him to come back. I have even gone into my Dad's things and started going through his work load, I think I might be better suited to that family business than this one. Tonight, I'm going to make my first kill since Eiran and I feel the adrenaline already, I need to be who I am, and that's a killer. The very idea of blood has me more excited than it should, I always believed I was not a killer at heart, but that my father loved to make me do it. It is in my veins, my very essence is murder, and he was right, walking away is never an option. I was born into this world, I will exit it and pay the price for what I do. I'm a murderer, but I have something my family didn't give me. Rules. I will not kill just anyone. I have a heart and I intend to look after it.

Standing in the wind watching the container being packed, I start to roll through the files for tonight's kill. This one caught my eye, the images made me feel and if I am going to kill I will feel it. A father, an abuser, selling his babies on the internet, a rapist. His wife has caught him and doesn't want to wait for justice that may not come, she's buying justice. My knife will judge him very harshly.

"We are ready to close it up, boss lady?" One of the loaders yells over to me. I nod and the container doors swing closed. I lock them myself and place numbered bullet seals through the latches.

"Get it to the stacks, here are the papers." I hand the forged documents to the truck driver's assistant and send them on their way.

I don't do back to the office, I just email Harmon the details of the shipment from my phone, I can't be asked to see him twice in one day. The images from this morning still have my stomach turning. I'm still using my father's car since I left mine to be stolen and I have no desire to shop for a new one. His work kit is still in the back even though he hardly killed anyone the last few years. I have double and triple checked it and added my knives to it. The cleaning team knows that they are on call tonight and I need this.

I drive to the beach nearest to where my target lives to wait for the cover of darkness. I park my car and sit on the bonnet to watch the sun go down over the ocean in front of me. My hair blows around my neck in the wind and I can smell the salt in the air, I close my eyes and breathe it in. I wish for it to be the mountain air and that I was back in Clarens with Mathew. My heart misses him so much. I can see his face in my dreams, feel my fingers in his hair and I can always smell him even though he is gone. Memories are interrupted by my phone ringing and I have the urge to hurl it into the ocean in front of me, but I hang onto it just in case Mathew wants to find me again. I hope. I know it's futile but I do.

The call is from Solly the man I have tasked with finding Harm's motives, I need to see his contract with Callum. Also they keep an eye on what he is up to. I don't trust the idiot at all.

"Talk to me," I answer the man in the hope he has news for me.

"I will have a copy of the amendment to you tonight." Oh he is good.

"How did you get it?" I dare asking.

"He seems to have upset one of the girls in the office today, I asked them before, but they were all mute. This afternoon she sent me a message to collect it after hours from her home for a fee." I laugh out loud, he really must be a shit lay. It can only be the whore from this morning.

"Pay her and tell her I will oversee her transfer to another department so she can be far from Harmon." I give him instructions.

"I was just going to kill her, boss?" So honest and efficient.

"Fine, it's cheaper, but I need clean up tonight too." I admire his work ethic.

"I will factor that in to my plans." He hangs up, not one for small talk, but I trust him, he has been on my father's payroll for years so he is loyal to me and not O'Reilly International. He's one of *mine*.

I'm in a hurry to get this done now so I can go home and read all about what it is Harmon is really doing here. I drive with the setting sun beside me up the coast to the affluent area where I will find daddy of the year. The surge of emotion is new to me and it's making this so much better than I ever had expected it to be. I know the man is home alone, I have the alarm codes and getting in and out is easy.

I'm in the house in no time at all, I can see him but he can't see me. He sits at his computer watching kiddie porn and drinking from a cheap brandy bottle. He is big and physically subduing him will be a challenge but I'm prepared. He gets up to take a piss, I notice he has no bottoms on, just the T-shirt. How disgusting. While he empties his bladder, I pour a little mixer in his drink and go into the next room to prepare for his departure from this life. I can feel the minutes counting down every time I hear the bottle bang back down on the table soon he will be ready for me. I wait just a few more minutes.

"Excuse me?" I call from behind him and he falls off the chair turning around to see me. I go stand over his body, cocking my head so I can look into his eyes I shake my head.

"Who are you?" he sputters out the words slurred and forced, the drugs claiming him.

"The Hummingbird." He looks confused.

"Hmm." He tries to lift himself off the floor and I take the moment to show him my knife. I slice off his exposed dick in a swift movement and drop it on the floor beside him. His screams are garbled and he tries to escape, worming around in his own blood.

"You shouldn't have used that on your kids," I say, my foot now on his forehead. The pool of blood is magnificent, I watch it getting bigger as he gets weaker and weaker. The crimson victory is painting a beautiful picture on the floor his hands are grabbing at his bloodied crotch and just before he passes out and can't feel anything anymore. I stand over his sick, sad pathetic body and slice his throat from one side to the other. No one has the ability to fuck us up quite like our parents and I feel like this is my way of fixing things. I wipe my knife clean on his T-shirt and go back into his spare room to pack my things and text the cleaners.

Crocodile farm. Male 100kg plus. I made a mess, sorry boys.

A few years ago my father bought the croc farm near the estate, it was a failing tourist attraction and the trade in skins and meat was lucrative so it was a good buy and a very convenient way to dispose of people. I get in the car and drive off into the night. No one's going to be sorry he's gone and that makes me feel good about it. I dial Mathew from the car. I know he won't answer, if he even still has that number but I leave a voice message.

"Hi, it's me. I did something tonight . . . I killed a man. I did it to save his children before it was too late for them. I miss you. I need the rules. You love me, I know you do. Come back. Please come back."

I hang up before he can hear my tears. I cry all the way home.

SOLLY IS WAITING FOR me in the driveway just outside the main gate to the estate, I stop next to his car and wind my window down. He hands me a memory stick and shakes his head. "She dead?" I ask just to make sure I don't need to call HR in the morning.

"Going to the crocs with your guy as we speak." He starts his car. "Avery, you need to deal with that." He points to the stick in my hand. "And fast." He sounds concerned and I feel the thick lead weight of dread as I swallow and nod.

"I'll handle it." I close my window and we drive on in opposite directions. I'm anxious to see what's on the drive but I need to wash the blood and the filth of the day off of me first. Once the car is in the garage and I have left my bags and bloodied clothing in the office, I run myself a bath. Now the memories of the tub are bittersweet and as I submerge myself completely under the water. I remember Mathew and what he taught me, I feel that the need to fight is about to become over powering. I sit up breaking the surface and breathing in, I miss him and that emptiness alone suffocates me some days, but it also drives me to live so I can find that feeling again. I dry off and slip into a tank top and yoga pants before I settle in front of my laptop, *mine* is secure and separate from O'Reilly International network. I plug in the usb and wait for it to open. I'm not a lawyer and the legal jargon is confusing but I get the jist of it and the more I read. I feel the bile coming up my throat, I gag and try to keep the sickness from escaping but I can't. *How could Callum do this to me? Why would he do it?* My fragile heart breaks as the betrayal sinks in and I digest the truth. I was just a way for him to get the one thing he needed but couldn't do himself. I feel hatred boiling up inside me, I *feel* it in every crevice of my soul. I know in all of this Mathew knew about this secret, he didn't tell me and that slaughters any bit of humanity I had. I learned from him that I need to fight, I don't need anything else. I will not give birth to another generation, I have said since I killed for the first time that this would all end with me—I am the last black hole heart. There will be no more. *I need a lawyer to translate all this shit, and I need Amya to see it too, because she's getting this company and I know she won't want it.*

There is almost no one I can trust, but Mathew said I could trust Owen, I just don't know now if I believe it, because he lied to me by leaving. His departure was a lie, he knew about this somehow, Callum must have told him. Callum lied to me and my father my whole life. I'm pretty sure this was his plan from the day he came home. He wanted to steal me to give him the heir that his poisonous wife wouldn't. Well I learned something from your story Callum, Shannon was right. I feel as if my whole life was a violation, I know my father didn't know about this because he was too busy being sad to notice his friend stealing his child. Callum manipulated us both, he was a living lie.

Anger's venom courses through me as I send a message to the number labeled Owen.

I need you, as a doctor. Mat said I could trust you.

I attach the location of the estate to my message and hope he comes or at least answers me.

It's 11pm do you want me to come now?
Yes I want you to come now.

On my way. Are you okay do I need to bring something with me?
Contraceptives, and an open mind.

He doesn't respond and I sit and wait for him to arrive. The anger turns to anxiety as I start to contemplate what lengths Harmon might go to. I won't let him rape me, inseminate me or put a baby in me by any means. I plan to kill him, but I need that deadline to expire first because if I read the legal shit right, if he dies before then the whole company goes to Amya and I would rather save her from this shit. I will call her tomorrow and discuss this shitstorm of a clusterfuck that's exploding around me. I dial Mathew again as I wait for Owen. I'm so angry with him now. Seething mad I growl into the phone.

"You knew all along what Callum had planned, you let me come home and walk into this. He could have raped me, kidnapped me, done anything to get what he wants and it would have been on you because you could have TOLD ME. You are like everyone in my life. I should have killed you the night I met you."

My angry words are yelled into the abyss of his voicemail as I cut the call and collapse on the floor and weep, I let myself love him and fuck me it hurts. Love will wound you far worse than any knife or gun in this world. I long for the ability to shut these feelings away in the vault of cold ignorance. I just want to stop hurting, this love in me is agonising.

An hour later, Owen rings the bell at the gate and I press the button to open it for him, his car tyres crunch the gravel driveway as I unlock the front door. He grabs a small black backpack off the backseat and walks towards the house, he looks rough like I woke him, who am I kidding, I woke him.

"Hi," he says with a sheepish look of guilt on his face. I suspect he knows at least part of this story already. He has what looks like bedhead and looks like morning after sex and before coffee.

"Get inside, there are people watching me all the time." I know they will be out there letting Harmon know that I had a visitor in the night.

He steps past me and I lock the gate and door again.

"I can't be here long, I have patient in labor so I have to get back." I didn't wake him, he was working. I almost feel guilty, but I don't really because I need to protect myself from this contract.

"I don't need you for long, I need contraception and to know some things." I usher him into the lounge area. "Coffee?" I ask him because I need some even if he doesn't.

"Yes please, black no sugar." Is there any other way to drink coffee?

"So, do you know his real name, Mathew that is?" I ask as I turn the coffee machine on and push the button to make two cups.

"Yes, we have been friends since junior school." He shakes his head and slumps his shoulders as he answers me.

"Look Avery, he came back here for Callum's case and it was awesome to see him after years, I know what he does and I accept and understand it. He can't plant roots. What he does is against the law and he will never stop. He's gone and I have no idea who you are and why he has this need to keep you safe so I'm just going to say this right now. I will not tell you who he is, I'm not giving you his name or where he went." I'm instantly irritated by him.

"I wasn't asking you to. I just needed to know that you also knew." I hand him coffee and sit opposite him.

"I need a contraceptive and I want a years supply of the morning after pill as the backup plan," I tell him.

"You don't need a contraceptive for another month, Mathew gave you a shot before he left it is good for three months. I can arrange the others for you." He still doesn't look me in the eye.

"He did what?" I'm confused.

"Fuck it all to hell, I might as well tell you what I know." He puts his cup down. "You obviously know some of it already."

"You better start talking before I start doing what I do best." I threaten him and put my gun down next to my cup. His eyes bulge and I can see his hand shake with fear, I like that he's afraid of me and can't help but smile.

"Mathew knew about this whole business of you having to get pregnant, he wanted to try and keep you safe, he was even going to stay, but the guy who's supposed to knock you up, tipped the cops off about him. He threatened him and you. He had to disappear. He told me the bits he knew and asked that if you needed help I help you and to break in here next month and inject you again." I'm sorry Owen has been dragged into this mess, but I do need him.

"He was going to stay?" That part stood out more than anything else.

"Yes, he said he felt like he found home." Owen sips his coffee his eyes on the gun and not me. I reach for it and he jumps a little as I get up and put it in the drawer. "He said that cops would bring attention to you, look I have no idea what it is you do but he seemed to think that it was better to just go." I sit again and contemplate the man in front of me, he isn't from our world, he's a good man, a bit of an asshole but a good man. He knows nothing about me, or people like me.

"You were going to break in here for him?" I raise an eyebrow and wonder how they ever thought that would work.

"I would have done anything for him. I owe him." I hear the sadness in his voice and I realise something despite the lies or truths.

"I owe him too." We finish our coffee in almost silence. I watch him and I see something I missed the first time we met it was hidden behind the ego. Owen carries a deep hurt in his eyes.

"Who ripped your heart out?" I sit back relaxed in his presence now.

"Love did, she's such a bitch." *She*–I laugh a little.

"That she is. My uncle taught me that if you love something you should kill it before it kills you. I'm beginning to see the truth in his words more every day." He looks genuinely shocked at my statement. I shake my head, he is not cut from the same bloodied rag as I am.

"Thank you for coming, Owen." I'm genuinely grateful, because I know more now. I know I'm going to kill Harmon O'Reilly and I'll love doing it.

"I will have your pills tomorrow, we can have lunch if you would like to get them from me?" I would have liked that but I cannot have Harmon knowing that I know what's going on and seeing an OBGYN would tip him off.

"I'll send a courier. Like I said, I'm watched all the time. I need to protect myself. Owen, tell him I understand." He smiles and shakes his head as he stands in the doorway of my home. I do understand it in a way. I feel less abandoned and more loved than I ever have in all my life. He left to protect me, he.

"Bye, Avery." He just puts a hand on my shoulder as he walks past me to his car.

HARMON

Ignorance is a voluntary misfortune.

A VERY HAS BEEN LESS hostile and I think being nice has started to pay off. I cannot rely on this happening naturally any longer and I have made a donation into a little white cup and have a plan to help the process along after the presidential event. I'm sure if I get her a little drunk and I can get physically close to her, I can convince her that we went to bed together. I may even go to bed with her if the doctor says it won't affect the results of the procedure. I had no idea the female body was quite that complicated. I have even had guys checking her trash so we could learn her cycle and that date is perfect for making a baby. Women are disgusting when you down to the biology of it.

My secretary left after I let her fuck me, she was obviously too delicate to work for me anyway. The new one is better at her job, all of it. She's better looking and more to my tastes, since I decided that there was no way to woo Avery I gave up and set my more forceful plan in motion so now I'm free to fuck the staff and anyone I want to really. I will have everything I want soon enough. I just have to convince her we had a one night stand and get her pregnant. I just hope we don't need to try more than once because my time is running out faster than I anticipated. I don't get it people have unwanted babies all the time and I am having no luck getting near her pants never mind getting her knocked up.

She has to be the most confusing human I have ever come across in all my days, at first I thought I would just tell her the plan and it would work but she loathes me, the open hostility may be gone but I can tell that she seethes with hate for me. I have come into her world and stolen her inheritance from her and it is hurting her. I secretly love the fact that it is, this was never her kingdom to rule she is *not* family no matter what my sad sick brother believed. I do, however understand that our child will be the purest form of monster ever born and that excites me, the possibilities for the future are endless. Callum's genius knew no boundaries and I have to admire that. He did underestimate the level of derangement that is Avery, I have been alerted to her latest extra-curricular activities and I have to say I'm impressed at how many bodies she is stacking up. The fascination lies in who she is killing, they are not even paying jobs some of them. She is acting as some sort of saviour for the wounded souls. She is becoming weak, soft and allowing emotion to affect her—she's going to get caught.

"What do you want, Baldini?" I answer the man's tenth call of the day.

"You know what I want you fool." He barks at me over the phone and I do know exactly what he wants. Revenge, he isn't done yet. Their family has no clue when to be done.

"I'm not done getting what I need from her. We discussed this."

"My patience won't last forever, I'm an old man and I would like to get this done before I die, boy." I made a deal with him, I give Avery in exchange and he leaves my family out of his vendetta. Now he is like a rabid dog with a bone. When he calls me 'boy' my blood pressure goes through the fucking roof and I'm reminded of my brother as I was abandoned at boarding school. *"Just behave boy, until I need you, your job is to behave."* I think he had this plan in his head even then.

He knew he would need me. I was needed, yet my whole life I had felt useless and pushed aside. I wasn't, he was just waiting for the right time, I am the one, the chosen one to make everything right again.

SOMETIMES IN OUR Lives we don't have the faintest idea what to expect, I didn't expect what I saw when I collected Avery from her room at the hotel on the evening of the presidents dinner. She was wearing a gown that exposed her chest and back, the black fabric highlights the vivid colours that adorn her milky white skin. The one side of her body is completely covered in tattoos, the side with her father's blue eye, the other side is white and pure—the opposite of her heart. The beauty of the monster before me is truly breath taking and when she takes the hand I offer her, I could easily fall prey to her seduction. I see how it was easy for her to kill so many men, they never stood a chance against that. My eyes take in every inch of her, usually she's covered and none of this exposed to anyone, I feel like she inviting me in just a little bit.

"You are so beautiful, Avery." I manage to let the words out softly in a whisper as she takes step towards me, her hand in mine. She is the most gorgeous woman I have ever seen.

"Looks can be very deceiving, Harm, but thank you." The villainous tone in her voice alerts me to just how difficult this might be, but I will do it by force if that's what it takes. Tonight I am putting a baby inside her, the future of crime families and the legacy my brother wanted so badly. We walk to the lift at the end of the corridor, my eyes catch the room where things are set up for after the event and my eyes linger on the number for a second. The doors close in front of us and for a few minutes as we descend, it is just me and her. We're looking back at ourselves in the mirror and I can see us in an alternate reality where we are the power couple in that image. The business man and the murderess, for a few minutes I think about what it would be like if I cared enough for one person to spend my life with them. To share my demons and fears instead I carry them alone. We look so normal in that reflection, a couple of young people off to a party in their finest clothes, but as she said looks are so deceiving. We are enemies beneath the surface.

I move so that I am standing a little closer to her and she moves her had to loop around my elbow, her shoulder brushes against mine and I feel the static electric shock of human contact. It makes me want to hold onto her, but I'm afraid to scare her and blow everything that is supposed to happen tonight, instead I bring my other hand up and brush her fingers slightly, she stiffens and her breathing changes so I stop right away. Something I notice now in this confined space is the absence of any jewellery, nothing adorns her except art. A woman like her has access to the finest diamonds on earth yet I have never seen her wearing a single one.

"No diamonds, or eccentric jewels to make the others jealous?" I look into her eyes but in the mirror as I ask her.

"Diamonds are filthy things." She answers with a sinister sneer on her face. "I would rather go naked than wear jewellery." Wow, note to self, don't bother buying her anything pretty.

"Hmm, you don't need them anyway." I remind myself to be nice and not let her see me judging her choices. I have embraced their way of doing things here the corrupt underhanded dealings, the disregard for the lives of anyone that isn't themselves so her choice surprises me. Cold blooded killing machine with a conscience. That thing I have always lacked, the ability to be sorry about my actions. I have never felt a connection or empathy to anyone, not just after my family were all killed, long before that I was an empty shell of a human. I see things differently, cleanly, without the tarnished emotion that others add to life. The doors open twelve floors down from where we got in, the ballroom is decorated in bold colours and gold everywhere. The guest list is a who's who of corruption and crime with a shiny exterior of business and the man in charge is here to announce his tenth wife. Politics is all about money and who has it. Money and power are two things I understand, unlike feelings and emotion.

"Can I get us a drink?" I ask her as we weave our way through the crowded room greeting adversaries, subsidiaries and partners along the way.

"Yes please, just water for me." No whiskey, no wine. *Shit, I had hoped she would get a little drink in her.* "You can cut all the crap, Harmon," she whispers. "My spies are better than yours." Sliding a hand down my chest and stepping into my personal space she has the devil in her eyes. "If we are going to make a baby, you should really start treating me like you want to be with me. I will give you what you need Harmon and then I'm out." This all seems too easy and I'm not sure how to react. When she leans right up against me and whispers, "This is where you pretend to have a heart and kiss me, you fucking idiot.People are watching us. We need to look like the power couple you want them to believe in." Fuck me she's good. I lean in and kiss her, I don't like kissing it's so personal, but when she kisses me back I forget my aversion to it and pull her into me. Avery tastes like everything I want.

The night passes with formalities, speeches, business talk and all I can think of is her and that kiss. I feel like I just sold my soul, she is so much better at this than I am. The people know her and love her, she's elegant and they all fall for her seductive ways. As the evening begins to wind down, the dance floor is opened and she gives me a death glare that tells me I better be a gentleman and ask her to dance. As I get up to do just that Baldini walks right up to her, they air kiss like old friends and she lights up with a smile as they greet each other. Before I can get to them he has whisked her away and she's dancing with the old man. How does she even know him, what is going on? I feel like I'm missing a giant piece of a puzzle. When Avery returns to the table, I'm quick to take her hand and lead her back to the dance floor, she melts against me as the music seems to possess her body.

My school ballroom lessons didn't prepare me for this and my body betrays me, I feel clumsy. Her perfume is seeping into my senses as we move across the polished wood floor, her dress ensures that no matter where I put my hands I am met with her soft skin.

"Are you ready to go upstairs, Harmon?" she asks into my neck as her fingers rake down the back of my tuxedo jacket.

"Are you going to kill me?" I have to ask, given her history.

"You and I both know that no one wins if either of us die before there is an heir to this blood stained throne, so no Harmon, I'm not going to kill you. I'm going to fuck you so we can get this over with." My mouth has gone dry and I'm sure I have been drugged, this is not the woman who has done nothing but avoid and hate me for almost a year.

"Let's go upstairs then." I smile as the words and reality come out of my mouth.

AVERY

Even the moon has a dark side.

A MYA SURPRISED ME when we met after I found out the ugly truth of what was the design for my future. She was efficient and had a lawyer there to look it over within hours, it turns out, I'm pretty much screwed until Harmon's grace period runs out. If he dies before then or vice versa, the company becomes Amya's. She wants no part of it and the thing about a crime conglomerate is you can't just sell it. But the lady is resourceful, she had a plan in place after only a few weeks, I didn't like that the plan included me having a relationship with Harmon and that I would have to have sex with him. The thought alone made me gag a little. The man is beautiful to look at, but he is just that and nothing more. After a little extra digging, I found out what he had planned, the idiot, and I decided to turn the tables on the imposter. After making sure with Owen that there was absolutely no chance of getting pregnant at all the plan was now in place, I would let Harmon know that I know, I would play the part, pretend that I agree and start a relationship with him. The power couple that the media and world needed to see. The company had taken a knock after Callum's death and this would bring us into the public eye in a good way. I have met the man who killed my father and wants my head on a golden platter, we have a truce, but things need to get better or it won't be worth his while. I will entertain Harmon until the deadline passes at which time Amya and I will sign the whole business over to him. I'll go back to my wine farm and she will disappear off the face of the earth again. Owen will play the part of fertility doctor and 'try' everything imaginable. I'm two steps ahead of Harmon and he's going to be very sorry he crossed me, the deceitful little prick.

On the night we are set to put the plan into motion, I have a minute where I feel the world is going to swallow me up and I will never come back from this. In that moment, I call Mathew and leave another message on his voicemail.

"I miss you, I'm about to break so many rules and it hurts without you. I have to fix this, I know you'll understand that. I need to feel like I'm more than just a black hole. God, Mathew. I'm going to bed with the fucking enemy tonight and all I can think of is that I wish it was you."

Watching Harmon's reactions as the night unfolds is priceless, it's better than any TV show I have ever seen, the shock and confusion is worth every minute that I am going to have to suffer in his presence. The little weasel has no clue who he's going up against and if he honestly thought his plan would work then I am dealing with a blithering idiot who has no place in this world. In fact, I'm amazed that no one has killed him yet. His eyes when Baldini asked me to dance made me smile, I don't often smile because life doesn't give me anything to smile at. I want to laugh at the ignorance, but I don't want to anger him yet. If he thought for one minute my staff and my almost friends would betray me and help him he was sadly mistaken, I have been part of this business my whole life. Sam however is swimming with the crocodiles tonight. The shit faced little worm.

When we have circulated and shown our ruse enough for the night, I ask him to go upstairs. He's afraid of me now, it's written all over his face. He's scared I will kill him. I am going to kill him—just not yet. First we need to be the most loved criminal couple in history, we need to be a united front and get the company back to its best or Baldini won't want it at all.

Before we leave the dance floor, I use the best weapon I have and push my body hard against his before I lean up and kiss him. Creating this kind of a public display of affection turns heads and has the Italian smiling. While I feel nothing from the connection but satisfaction of winning the game, I can tell that I affect him, not that he would ever tell anyone. I may just be the hammer that breaks his walls down, the cold empty man has a pulse after all, it's just in his pants.

"Let's go, Harmon." I keep telling myself to be believable. He may be a fool but I don't need my emotions getting me caught out.

THAT WAS THE MOST anti-climactic sex of my life. I think messing around with high school boys was more satisfying. He may look like man candy on a stick, but Harmon can't back it up in bed. I may be jaded and I was comparing him to Mathew the whole time. Once in my life I liked my men to lay down behave and let me take over, but now I need more than that. I need the thrill of losing control and I had all the control, it's me in the driver's seat now and I don't like it.

"This is not how I had planned this all to happen," he says to me as I slide out of the bed and away from his still naked body.

"Oh, I know that. You really think that your stupid plan would have worked?" He really is a fool, the more I look at him the dumber he seems to get.

"I had to do something." He lifts himself up on his elbows and I can see the visual appeal as his smooth chest is on display.

"And not once did you think let me discuss this with her like a person? You know I'm a person, what did you think I would do when I found out? I knew your brother was insane. The madness in that man knew no limits." It's the truth, he killed his whole family, married a crazy woman and tried to steal me from my family. He was certifiable.

"You didn't exactly make it easy to talk to you." He has a point.

"I don't play well with assholes, Harmon, simple, you acted like an entitled dick." We better just get this all out in the open since we are going to be fucking. "I have been here my whole life, I lived, breathed and murdered for him. Then you just appear as he is ready to die, excuse me for being upset." I pull out a pair of jeans and a sweater from my suitcase across the room.

"I was locked away after he murdered our whole family and then he chose you to be the *special one* when I was his blood. Forgive me for not liking you, but I am entitled to this, Avery. This company has my name on it, not yours." He sits up and faces me now, I wish he would cover up. "I will be damned if I lose it all now." The subtle threat in the last sentence isn't missed. I leave the room and go shower and get dressed, locking the door between us. I secretly hope he leaves to his own room since he has nothing in here.

As the water cascades over me, the bathtub taunts me with memories, some horrific and others haunting my heart with the images of love and fighting. I feel the tears start to fall. I've betrayed what I had with Mathew and tainted it with Harmon. I should kill him, but then Baldini would kill me. My whole body aches for the love he showed me. I sob quietly in the shower while I try to scrub Harmon off of me. He smells like a lawyer and I'm sure this is a signature scent that they bottle just for them. It's vile. The more I wash myself, the sicker I feel about this. I don't want to be with him, I don't even want to be near him. Puking up the expensive dinner I ate earlier, I feel the slightest bit better as I remind myself that I am doing this to end it all. The Italian can have it and I'll be free. I'm desperate to break this vicious cycle, to put an end to crime families. There should be no crime in a family the whole term is just wrong on the most basic level. You cannot have both things, I cannot be a killer and have a family—I won't. When I emerge from the bathroom at least an hour later, he's still here, at least he has pulled his pants on now, but I notice the complete absence of tattoos on his body. A vision of Eiran's back flashes through my mind as I take in just how out of place this man is in my world. I have no doubt that he is mentally as fucked as his brother but his demons are all on a leash, he has yet to lose his cold collected facade and come alive. His madness has been kept in a cage.

"I ordered coffee." He points to a cup on the small table. As if I would drink anything left unattended with him.

"No thanks." Frowning, he turns away to answer his phone and I slip on my shoes and leave him, alone in my hotel room.

There is an eerie silence at this hour of the morning, not everything is sleeping but nothing is waking up yet. I stroll through the hotel gardens, missing Jameson who's staying with Amya and Robin this weekend. Owen claimed that the dog hates him. There is a quiet bench in the corner of the formal gardens where I sit, staring at my phones lock screen where Mathew and Jameson look back at me and I feel lost. I dial his number, it is always the same digital voicemail message that greets me when all I long for is his voice.

"I love you, Not Mathew. When all this chaos is over, I'm going to find you. My reason and season are not over, I fucking love you and that's a reason."

I leave the teary angry message and hang up, I'm going to fill his mail box soon if I don't stop doing this. I'm a fool leaving messages for a man that said he didn't love me. I spill my tears and hope for a future that I'm certain I cannot have. I scroll through my messages and emails sitting in the predawn light, it all seems so unnecessary now that I know there are other things to life. I wonder if that's what my mom felt like when she had her little café and a husband she loved. I often ask myself if I was the reason things changed, if my birth was just the preface to her end, maybe it was my fault. She protected us by dying, I know my Dad told me over and over, but the letters she left me made me feel as if it was more. Their love story is so tragic that I think it over shadowed my whole life.

The sun is almost up by the time I get back to my room. I had to stop at reception and get a key because I locked mine inside and I was hoping he was gone and knocking wouldn't help. I miss my home, coming inland and away from the vineyard and ocean makes me feel trapped. I open the door to the hotel room determined to pack my things and get to the airfield early I will take the company plane home, we flew here on separate planes so I have no issue leaving alone. I can't do this all at once, I already have the urge to slice him open and watch him bleed out.

Picking up last night's clothing off the floor, I feel the urge to puke again, the memories of Harmon's hands touching my body make every cell in me revolt. The creepy feeling he caused as his fingers traced the line down my chest and the disconnected emptiness of his kisses. There's absolutely nothing behind his actions, not a single feeling, I wonder if I felt like that to them all before Mathew. Was I missing from my body?

There are too many things invading my thoughts and I want to run again.

I'M SITTING IN THE small private jet looking out of the window at the pretty pilot as she flirts with the co-pilot jealousy ripples down my spine. I accept that I will never be normal, that my life will not be hearts and daisies. That doesn't stop the desire for those things from gripping onto me and choking my heart. *Not long and I can walk away, I may not find normal but I will find peace. This inner turmoil and pain that has clung to my life has got to end.*

A surge of anger comes over me as I see Harmon walking towards the steps of my aircraft. Fucker. He has this look of 'I win' all over his morning after unshaved face and I want to slap it right off, because he didn't win me. I'm sacrificing myself to that fucking devil. Thank the good Lord the flight is less than two hours, I will pretend to sleep or read a book, anything but Harmon sounds appealing this morning.

He sits in the seat directly infront of me facing me with his shit eating grin and smooth business man look, but before he does he leans down and pecks me on the cheek like we are lovers. I snarl at him, because I don't have actual words, he's delusional. I will play nice in public and fuck him into believing I'm trying to have a baby but I don't play house. I close my eyes and feign sleep until I feel the wheels hit the ground in Cape Town.

HARMON

Love: the delusion that one woman or man differs from another.
~ Henry Louis Mencken

NEVER ONCE DID it occur to me to just tell the truth. I was so caught up in deceiving her that I didn't consider that she might just see the reason behind this plan. Her willingness not only to embrace the idea of us having a child but to create an *us* for all to see is genius. The image of a power couple running this ship could be what we need to pull out of the free fall we are in. I watched her pretending to sleep on the way back, she was all covered up. No sign of the artwork that was displayed the night before, just the same her I've seen for the past few months. I have the urge to touch her, brush my knuckles across her cheek, rest my hand on her thigh, or maybe kiss those lips again. There is an indescribable feeling the first time you kiss someone, not an emotion, a physical response. It is never the same after the first time, but with her I want to try and make it the same. A deep need for her to be mine is starting to rear its head, I want her to be my *possession, my asset, just mine.* Then I want her to give it all to me everything that always should have been, everything my brother took from me and gave to her. I want to leave her with nothing just so she needs me.

When we landed, she was cold and distant again. This is the Avery I know. Not like she had been in front of all those important people or when we were in bed, the seductress was now just the bitch again. I don't like it, she needs to learn that this is a serious business relationship. I let her be until work the following morning when she comes in like a whirlwind barreling through the place, barking orders, yelling at people and threatening staff with death, I have never seen her with such fire in her.

"Harmon, boardroom on the third floor in fifteen minutes," she yells at me as she passes the door of our office it is only then that I notice almost all of her stuff is missing the desk is devoid of her clutter. Not sure how I'm supposed to respond to her yelling and bossing I just sit at my desk and stare at the empty one, what is she doing?

"Harmon." She's standing in the doorway, her cheeks are a little flushed and her eyes are alive with something new. "Harmon."

"Yes." Shit. My head is a mess looking at her.

"I have moved to Eiran's old office and we have a meeting in ten with two of our Middle Eastern suppliers." She spits the information at me in a hurry and starts to walk away, scrambling for my jacket I rush to follow her.

"Why are you moving office? What's the meeting about?" I ask chasing her down the corridor to the lift at the back of the building.

"Because I don't want our new personal relationship to affect how this business needs to be run, and it's about weapons, the trafficking of humans and some very sought after Burmese rubies. Any other stupid questions before we go in? Do you read your email or play games on that computer all day?" She glares at me with one eyebrow raised and I feel like that kid in boarding school again.

"I liked sharing an office and I didn't get an email. Also I spend all day balancing finances, fending off numerous legal issues and licking the asses of the entire countries ruling party." I do work, I may not have my hand in all the dealings like she does but I have other crap on my plate. Namely her up until now.

"Shut up, just sit in here act like we love each other and let me get this done." She stands so close I can smell her, her eyes bore into mine as she makes clear where the power lies right now.

"Fine, why am I even here then?" She kisses my cheek as a man in a suit and too much aftershave passes us and whispers in my ear.

"Because we are a team remember, the mob family to rule them all. Wake up, Harmon." She straightens my already straight tie and follows the man into the boardroom, she is wearing pants and long sleeves today. Very corporate and very modest. Her hair is pulled up in a long ponytail that swings to the same rhythm that her heels click along the floor. My eyes stay firmly planted on the way her ass moves as she walks and I stroll behind her and I smile as she flips her middle finger at me behind her back. This is her kingdom and she rules it very well.

THE MEETING DRONES on for what seems like a lifetime, and even more so since they don't speak English I had no idea that she speaks other languages. I sit there watching and I wonder how many she speaks? They seem to be arguing now and Avery just sits back and lets them, she doesn't engage in their hostility, but watches it very carefully. In the end, they all shake hands mine included and the meeting is adjourned, I have no idea what any of it was or why I was in there but I am no better or worse off for it. After the last of our guests is in the lift and the doors close separating them from us she turns to me,

"You did okay. You don't speak Arabic do you?" I shake my head, no most people from Ireland don't. "I have other work to do, then we need to have a little discussion you and me." No fake kisses or close contact she just opens the fire escape door and takes the stairs back up to our floor. I wait for the lift to return and take it downstairs instead. I need a decent cup of coffee and I need to go to the pharmacy. The small coffee shop across the street makes a reasonably good latte and I walk the block down to a small retail centre that has a pharmacy. Sipping the warm coffee, I wander past the shelves full of drugs, shampoos, body lotions, bandages and nutritional supplements until I find what I'm looking for. Pregnancy tests, folic acid and a pre-natal vitamins and an ovulation kit—everything listed on the tips for getting pregnant fast website. The man behind the counter gives me the eyeball as he rings it all up and shoves it in a brown paper bag. With the bag in my hand, I walk back to O'Reilly International head office and get some work done. Mostly I work with legal papers like contracts and such, todays little negotiation while foreign was rather refreshing for me.

My new assistant is in and out with papers and messages, she doesn't look at me or make a move in my direction. The other female staff members have all flirted a little, she's just business and nothing else. I grab her hand as she takes my empty coffee cup, she whips it away gives me a death glare and grinds out. "I like girls, Mr O'Reilly." I'm a little turned on by her statement, maybe she can be a little challenge since Avery isn't one any longer.

Avery comes into the office a little before four in the afternoon, she has rolled up her shirt sleeves and her hair is now twisted up in a knot.

She doesn't sit down behind her old desk instead she sits on it, her legs dangling off the edge one crossed over the other at her ankles. I see her smile, I imagine it to be genuine and that she might actually like me beneath the bitch face and control freak. I want her to like me, but no one ever really likes me.

"Here is how this works, Harm." Her voice is so smooth that the hostility is lost on me. "We appear together when needs be, I'm not your girlfriend. I won't be shacking up with you, I'm not going to hold your hand and kiss your ass." She jumps off the desk and stalks towards mine, leaning over and putting her pretty manicured hands in front of me. I swallow the giant lump she caused, thankfully she can't see the state of my cock right now. "We will fuck during my fertile days to try and make this wonder child your brother so desperately wanted, I'm not going to cuddle you or sleep next to you all night. This is *not* that." She gestures between us.

Not really, I have no clue why but I want more than that. I wouldn't dare tell the knife wielding bitch that though, I'll work up to that. I had an image in my mind of us being a happy little family. The ever after that Callum never got.

"I'm sure I can make it work." A frown furrows her forehead as she gives me a genuine death glare. Did I say something wrong?

"Harmon, you don't know me well enough to understand that whatever little fairytale you have in that stupid head of yours is never going to happen. So stop thinking it and accept that this is how it is. I'm in charge now, you tried and failed to get the better of me." Her words are like acid as she spits them at me. "God I hope this kid gets my brains, because there's something wrong with yours." The insult hits me right in the gut, I have always been considered clever, or above average until I came here and had to decipher this world where crime, violence and emotion is all mushed together. *I'm not dumb, I'm horribly confused, bitch.* This world they have created is pure insanity, I preferred the one where I existed amongst people who had no fucking idea who I was and I only had to interact with them when I wanted to. I was blissfully alone, with a stupid whore to fuck at night. Callum was correct, she was a whore. This is so frustrating.

"Fine, Avery, whatever you say. How will I know what days are shagging days then?" My interpersonal skills are not the best when I am irritated.

"Give me your phone, there's an app for that." Is she for real, an app? I can see the 'what the fuck' rolling into my eyes like a slot machine. "I will sync mine to your phone that way you can know when it is optimal." Clinical and emotionless, she speaks about this like it is nothing to her, unlike when she spoke of her father or Mathew or even work, she doesn't care about this. I need to make her care more. This has to work. A pink app square appears on my screen and there is a little flower in the notification bubble. I just look at it, afraid to open it. I don't really want to know about periods and ovulation I want to have sex like we did because it was damn good.

"Flower means we are good to go. And Harmon, one other thing, while we are doing this you do not put your dick in anyone else. I do not want to catch a disease and you need to save your sperm for baby making. If I find out you are fucking anyone else then this arrangement is over." I can hear the threatening tone that rumbles through her as she stands up and straightens her skirt.

"Avery, I cannot survive on five days of sex a month." I'm being honest. I need the release to keep from my own insanity.

"You have a hand and I know for a fact that you went quite a while without any when you got here, just get used to it. I'm not your girlfriend, wife or whore." Before I can rebut she has slammed my office door and left me feeling as if I have my pants down.

No sooner has the sound of the door slam disappeared and my phone buzzes with a message notification.

Tonight, I will come to you since leaving seems so very difficult for you.

God she is the most infuriating bitch I have ever come across, I hate that she's controlling me. I hate that she can, but I can't exactly make my own baby. Can I? I start to think about it and type the words into my Google search and comb through the results.

AVERY

Just as a snake sheds its skin,
we must shed our past over and over again.

THE FIRST MONTH was the hardest, I had to fight my gag reflex as I pretended to enjoy having sex with Harmon as much as he seemed to be enjoying it. I felt like my soul was dying every time, I would try and just focus my mind elsewhere, but switching my emotions off was no longer an option for me. I felt this, I get my grief and my pain and everything else as I continued to keep him just happy enough that the idiot wouldn't do anything stupid. Babysitting him is a full time job that is sucking the life out of me, he even Googled whether or not he could have a baby on his own. The man is insanely clever at what he does, numbers and legal shit, but good God he's as thick as pig shit about anything that requires him to understand humans on any level. The second night of this torture, I went to his flat and after sex he handed me a package of prenatal vitamins, ovulation and pregnancy test. I wanted to hold him down and stick them down his throat and leave him to die choking on them, the hatred that I had for him was growing into a very serious animal that I was going to have to keep on a leash.

Today, he's coming with me to see Owen, my gyno because he can't understand why I am not pregnant yet, his ignorance is helping this plan along nicely. When we spoke on the phone about this Owen laughed with me and I can say that the man might just be the only friend I have in the world. We have a plan. This time, he will talk to Harmon about how hard it is to actually get pregnant, hoping this will give us another month or two. I drive us to the very upmarket woman's health centre where Owen works. A place where the walls are decorated in vagina pictures and posters about laser vaginal rejuvenation are proudly displayed, a place that would make any man cringe. I must admit I'm going to enjoy watching the physical reaction I know that Harmon will have. It is time to take sex education to a whole new level. I have watched him drowning in his own delusions the last three months, the man is a mental patient waiting to happen. I have made sure that he is under ten ton of work pressure, creating problems that don't even exist to keep him distracted and stressed to the maximum. He has even lost that look of refined gentleman. He looks frayed and a little lost. I park right in front of the door and when he comes to stand next to me the smell of his cologne is overwhelming. I side step a bit, but he reaches out and holds my hand. We are in public, he thinks we should appear to be a couple. I want to rip my hand away and punch him in the nut sack. I have to remind my body not to obey my mind. I cannot help but smile at what he's about to walk into as we push open the giant mirror glass doors our reflection evaporates and is replaced by a reception desk and the biggest vajayjay you have ever seen in your life framed and hung on the wall behind it. I glance sideways to see Harmon swallow as he adjusts his tie and sticks his hand in his pocket. The one holding mine has gone clammy, it's disgusting but so satisfying.

"Avery for Dr. Owen," I say to the lady seated below the painting.

"Hi, yes down that passage to right you can check in with his receptionist there." She points and I drag him with me as we walk down the hall of horrors for any guy, pictures like the one up front are all over the place. When we get to Owen's practice rooms I'm greeted by his receptionist, she smiles and calls Harmon my husband which he enjoys entirely too much to correct her, so I do.

"Oh, this is Harmon, he's not my husband." The girl blushes and apologises and I can see the steam of my blatant rejection coming out of his ears. His ego is not used to me yet, and I enjoy bruising it so much.

"I'm so sorry, have a seat I will call you when the doctor is ready for you." She motions to the chairs arranged around the room, which is surprisingly quiet, bar a pregnant lady and her husband sitting in the one corner. I take the opportunity to remove my hand from his as we sit down to wait. Lesson one, Harmon, the gyno is never on time, ever. After half an hour, he's tapping his foot annoyingly and the couple who was ahead of us has just been called so we will still be waiting a bit. I flip the pages of a magazine I'm not reading and try to focus on the present when my mind still drifts to the past, to Mathew, to the rules that I'm breaking every day. This is hurting me and more than I want to admit. A heavy sadness settles in my belly as we get called back to his exam room, also known as the place where dignity goes to die.

"Avery, Harmon, come in take a seat." Owen's friendly voice and outstretched hand greet us at the door, but his eyes are asking me if I am okay. I nudge Harmon who looks concerned by the fact that my doctor could be on the cover of GQ, he looks him up and down a few times and looks at me eyes full of 'have you fucked him' questions. Which can be answered with 'he is still alive isn't he?'

"What can I help the lovely couple with today?" Owen is sugar sweet. The fake smile he wears hides his disgust for Harmon well. I look at Harmon letting him know he needs to answer that, he is the one that's all worried about this. He stutters and has to try twice before words form and he asks.

"We are trying to have a baby and she isn't falling pregnant." So eloquent, idiot. I cannot hide the look on my face thankfully he is looking at Owen and not me.

"Well, falling pregnant can depend on many factors, not just Avery. It is also not as easy as the world would have you believe there is only really a twenty-five percent chance of getting pregnant each cycle. Those are not the best odds." He talks to him like he is a child in grade school, I secretly enjoy it so much.

"Avery, let's get you on the table do an exam, run some tests to rule out any problems then we can discuss some options, but I don't recommend anything more than trying until that hasn't worked for a year." Harmon eyes bug out at the mention of a year.

"We don't have a year." He snaps. Owen looks at him like he is mad.

"Harmon, I am not God, I can only try and help you." The sarcasm is seeping out.

The true nature of just how delusional Harmon is about us are coming out during this exam, he turned puce when Owen asked me to undress and put on a gown. He developed a twitch in his jaw when Owen did the breast exam. The jealous rage in his eyes was almost too good to be real. Most doctors wouldn't invite the man into the exam, but Owen knew what I was trying to do and played along so perfectly. I have to say it did feel strange to be naked and on display for my friend. I keep reminding myself this is his job, he looks at vaginas all day every day. This isn't personal.

"I need to take a swab for a pap smear and I would like to do an internal ultrasound to rule out cysts, endometriosis and fibroids as possible issues." Owen talks to me as if Harmon isn't in the room about to explode with rage. I nod and lay down on the table. "Move all the way to the edge of the bed and put your feet in the stirrups for me," he says, clicking them into place. My eyes are focused on Harmon, because I would rather watch his horror than my friend getting up close with my vagina. Harm mouths to me, "What the hell?" I just smile and nod like all this is normal. He breathes out loudly through his nose, snorting with disgust as his eyes catch the speculum and he cannot hold it in any longer.

"What is that?" he asks, eyes like saucers.

"I place this inside the vagina and open it gently so that it is held open and I can take a swab and examine the cervix." Owen is all doctor. This is uncomfortable for him too. The lubricated torture implement is pushed inside me as I undergo a totally unneeded exam. I stare at the ceiling and try not to think how much this would hurt Mathew, I don't want him to know about this ever. I left him a voicemail this morning, but after all this time I have almost given up hope that he gets them. I can hear the sound of the plastic crackling and the loud gasp the Harmon allows to escape, he is holding my hand like he is marking territory. To be honest, I'm surprised he hasn't pissed on me just to show Owen I am his, even if it's in his head only.

"This may be uncomfortable, Avery. You can see the display there on the monitor." He points for Harmon to look. As my insides are displayed for them to see I realise just how dangerous the game I'm playing is, Harmon is not in his right mind. I swallow a small lump of fear as the discomfort of this is overpowered by the sudden fight or flight reflex. This plan is stupid. I need to find a better way of doing this and soon. He's bound to get desperate and do something idiotic.

Owen made it very clear to Harmon that there is nothing wrong with me and that if we haven't made a baby in two months he should get tested. He took the time to tell him that his smoking, drinking and underwear choice could all be affecting his little swimmers. I had to bite my tongue to stop the laughter escaping when the horror was painted over his face. Yes, Owen just insulted your manhood without you even noticing.

THE DRIVE BACK TO the office was both satisfying and painful. He put his hand on my thigh and left it there, like he was my lover. He was being possessive of something that doesn't belong to him. The conversation was not much better.

"He shoved those things inside you, is that even allowed?" I could hear the jealousy in his voice as his foot tapped on the floor mat. "I mean, surely he can't just touch you there."

"What did you imagine a gynecologist did, Harmon?" I'm truly shocked at his ignorance for a man who googled insemination and was ready to have his doctors knock me up.

"I don't know, but that just seemed so . . . umm . . . intimate. I mean he grabbed your boobs." I want to laugh but I am concerned at this jealousy, instead I pull over into a service station so Harmon and I can chat for a minute. "What are you doing?"

"Stopping so we can have a little talk, because you're losing your shit." I snap at him as I forcibly remove his hand from my leg. "Firstly Harmon, he is my doctor. It is not the first or the last time he will shove his equipment in me, that's his job. Second you wanted to go with me, because you don't trust me, because you have deluded yourself making this more than what it is. I'm not yours, Harmon, I don't belong to you. I have fucked other men and I will continue to do so when this is over. You are just lucky that I haven't killed you yet. Get this picture of you and me out of your head. This isn't my fault. You heard the doctor, there is *nothing* wrong with me. You are probably shooting blanks."

"I am NOT firing blanks, you bitch." He loses his short temper with me grabbing my jaw in his hand forcing me to look into those empty eyes. Only now can I see the insanity in him, the madness that lived in his brother is right there below the surface and he's losing control of it. "I can't do this your way Avery, I can't have him or anyone touching you, fuck. How do I know you aren't fucking him?" There it is the insecurity that rules his weak mind. "When he touches my boobs, it's to check for cancer, you know that disease that killed your brother, but you didn't give a shit about Callum. You didn't watch him die slowly." I sigh loudly. "I'm not fucking him, he's my doctor. You don't have a choice about how we do this, because I am the one with the womb you idiot." I pull my head back escaping his grip. "Harmon you need to get a grip, because I have money and I can live quite happily without this company. I'm doing this for you, not me." His jaw ticks, and his pupils dilate with rage as he grabs me leaning closer again. Fear pricks at my mind, he's becoming a danger to me. His lips touch mine, I turn to ice. His tongue swipes at mine and my mouth feels like I swallowed ash. He tries to pull me closer still and I go stiff in defense.

"I want you so much it's all I think about, Avery. Don't you understand the life we could have," he says with his head rested against mine. *Fight.*

"I have a life Harmon, you need to get your own. This fantasy will never come to life." I shove him back to his seat and start the car again. When we get to the office I leave the car on for him to get out, I need to go and see the manager at the croc farm to sign the new license to trade in skins.

"Are you not coming up?" Harmon looks at me as he clicks his seatbelt open.

"No, I have things to do." He gets instantly angry,

"But you are ovulating, I'll just come with you."

"I'll still be ovulating later, I promise." I'm in no mood for this.

"Then we can do it again then." He snaps and puts the belt back on, I have upset his little world.

"You know that this company you are so desperate to have doesn't run itself, you actually have to work." I bite at him as I speed out of the parking again. I don't need this now. He is being petulant.

"You never work," he whines like a child that was told to pack up his toys.

"I'm always working, Harmon. Always." It's the truth, I don't get to be off from work because this work is my life—for now. This field trip might be the reality check he needs. The drive from the city to the Francshoek Valley is about an hour if no one has caused a traffic jam. That hour of silence with him huffing and puffing next to me felt like a year, I eventually turned the music loud enough to drown him out and let my mind drift to another time.

The first time I came to the croc farm, I was in awe of the beasts that could crunch bones and so easily dismember a body, my father brought me to show me our newly acquired assets. It was muggy and hot, crocs don't smell nice, the green water in their dams combined with their shit was vile and it hung in the air. We'd killed a man the night before, one of the many times I worked with my dad as a team learning to hone my skills. The body was in the back of the car, this was the first time we were going to see if this was an effective means of disposal. I watched them all laying in the sun on the grass embankment, warming their cold-blooded bodies. I thought they looked so menacing even with their eyes closed asleep you could tell they were the villains. Two men helped us drop the body into the rank green water, no sooner had the splash been hard there was a frenzy, chaotic movement as they all swarmed it. Within minutes it was ripped apart and consumed, all of it even his head was gone. What a brilliant thing nature is.

"Where are we going?" Harmon asks me disrupting the memory, one where I had actually enjoyed the day with my father.

"To one of my properties. I told you I had shit to do." I grind the words out between my gritted teeth. I hate Callum for this right now, I feel like everything he and I shared was based on this monumental lie. The thought of him makes me feel used and violated. Not even being raped felt like this, the betrayal of the man I spent my life idolising has almost destroyed me and even now I'm living with the ghosts of his madness. It's no wonder his wife killed him, had I known the truth I would have killed him instead of offering a part of me to save his life. Just thinking of him makes my anger burn with a new heat and his little brother beside me is feeding the monstrous rage in me allowing it to consume me.

I park in the dusty parking area outside the staff entrance to the farm, as I open the doors the smell I am now used to fills my nostrils and I hear a gag from Harmon. It is not pleasant here, this place is a barbaric reminder of the cruelty of life.

"What is this place?" he asks covering his mouth and nose.

"Crocodile farm, I don't just farm wine my interests are diverse." I glare at him and smile, the smell no longer an issue for me.

"What on earth do we have farm crocs for?" *We* the word out of his mouth makes me want to spit.

"Not *we*. This is *my* farm Harmon, it has nothing to do with you or O'Reilly International. My father bought it for me to help get rid of my toys." I make the purpose of this place very clear, "Our business tends to produce a vast number of dead bodies, they're not easy to get rid of. This place is one of the ways we make them disappear." I talk as we walk towards the big wooden gate that will take us into the back of the farm, the commercial part. The other side of the property is disguised as a tourist attraction. He has no words, he just follows me inside where Edgar greets me with a big smile. He runs the farm and has a creepy infatuation with the animals.

"Avery, so glad you are here." He reaches out a hand for me to shake and his yellowing teeth are bared to me in a smile.

"Edgar, this is Harmon O'Reilly. I came to sign the new license application quickly."

"Hi." He gives Harm the once over and clearly doesn't like him. "Sure. Let's pop into my office and sign it. I need to supervise feeding at the number four pen in twenty minutes if you two want to watch?" I step into the small office, the old furniture is permanently imbedded with the stench of crocodile.

"I would love to." I know what that means and seeing the stuck up office boy witness feeding will be so much fun. I see Harmon about to open his mouth and speak but he obviously decides to shut it. I sign the documents that are put in front of me and he finally chimes in.

"Are you even going to read those, you just sign things blindly, Avery. That could be anything." He snatches the papers and starts to read them, I know what they say because I have signed them since I was eighteen and this place became legally mine. I don't need to read them. Looking sheepish he hands them back to me without a word after he has read them through.

"It's a licence to trade in skins, Harmon, not an agreement for organ trade or sex slaves." My claws are out today.

"Okay, let's go feed the babies," Edgar says grabbing his big chain of keys. It jingles like a jailer as he walks out ahead of us. The long maze of wooden bridges are erected over the pens below give us a view of the nearly six thousand crocs we have here at any given time. Crocs need copious amounts of food and we get ours from local farmers, chickens, cows and sheep—who cares—as long as its dead they'll eat it. Today, there's a huge plastic bin filled with chickens that have passed the sell by date and then some, they're ripe and I can smell them a good way off. Two farm hands are waiting for us at the small gate that opens into the pen, a big number four is painted on the gate, these crocs are four years old and almost ready to be slaughtered. Different ages for different purposes, handbag crocs die younger than paté crocs. The younger they are, the softer their skins. We make a fair profit off the meat as well, after tasting it I can't understand how though.

"Okeeeey jullie twee gaan in en passop." Edgar sends the two men in and warns them to be careful, one has a large stick in his hand and the other lifts the large bin and carries it behind him. Edgar is holding a hunting rifle in his hand just incase they get out of hand. They empty the drum, some in the water, some on the grass and then make a quick exit as the animals turn from lazy sun basking beasts to barbaric savages tearing into the meat.

"I wonder how many of my lovers those crocs have had the pleasure of eating?" I say loud enough for Harmon to hear me. Looking him the eyes, I don't need to say more my intentions are clear, this is where he will find his end. I only hope it is soon, because I can't be nice much longer its killing me.

"Thank you, Edgar, I will see you soon." I put my hand on his shoulder and say goodbye, I like the old man he doesn't judge and I can trust him to do his job quietly.

I'm tired of playing by the rules of someone else's game, I need to find a better way to end this shit.

"What now? We have business to attend to, Avery." Harmon pulls me into his chest as we get to the car and I have to swallow my own vomit. Best get it over with.

"You can come with me to the estate, but you are leaving when we are done, Harmon." I spit and shove him away from me, the crocodile smell is less offensive than his aftershave.

"How am I supposed to leave, we're in your car?" The whining again.

"I have another car at the estate and a driver who can chauffeur your ass home, Harmon. You. Are. Not. Staying." I slam my door waiting for him to get into the passenger side.

NOT MATTHEW

There is no fear for one whose mind is not filled with desires.

WHEN MY SISTER died, I missed her like only a twin could miss their other half. I cried, I got angry, I yelled and then I made myself a promise. I would do my best to stop the suffering of others, those I could not save, I would help them end their suffering. Yet, here I sit and nothing can soothe the pain in me, I cannot put to rest the ache in my heart. I may have saved her but I sacrificed myself in the process, I was going to stay. I wanted to try and make her world perfect as it always should have been. Waking up with her next to me, going to bed knowing she's mine. Harmon had other ideas, his little tip off to the police has turned my life into a series of disasters that have taken far too long to fix. The Italian made it go away, but I have to stay away until he has what he wants from Avery. I'm not privy to what that is. He did swear a lot and call Harmon some less than favourable names in Italian, it would seem that he likes him even less than I do. By the time he was done ranting about him, the man's face was red and he had beads of sweat on his forehead. You see, cancer has no loyalty. It takes anyone it wants without consideration and the balding man with a blood thirst for revenge has a son who he would give anything to save—even give up his revenge. When he muttered about Rowan killing his brother I automatically corrected him, it was not something I thought about directly, it came out my mouth. "But Callum killed Renzo." His eyes went wide and grabbed my shirt pulling me right up to his face.

"What did you say?" He fumed at me.

"I said, Callum killed your brother, Lauri begged Rowan in her final letter to him not to kill him, she wanted hers to be the last death in that feud." He looks at me like I am talking alien. "Who told you it was Rowan?" I'm now intrigued and as confused as he is. I'm an outsider and I know that, Callum and Avery both told me the story of how he came home.

"Harmon." I should have known that would be his answer.

"Look, that dip-shit is an idiot. Callum told me himself about killing Renzo, about how his body was scarred and that he had asked him to kill him." The old man looks at me shakes his head and the rage is replaced with sadness.

"My father hated Renzo and Renzo he never let all that anger go. He did some horrible things you know." He sighs and sits down in the big leather chair behind him.

"Look, I'm not part of this crime family web of lies and murder. I got here by falling in love, I can say that I think it is time to end it all now. I will do everything I can to save your son, because I can see in your eyes that you love him. Let this revenge go, enjoy what time you have left, hate is not what you should be spending your time on."

"The girl is no longer in my sights, I will hold her to our agreement to merge companies so that she may return what my brother wrongfully gave to her. You are a very wise young man you know?" He wipes his brow with a hanky and pulls a cigar out of his pocket.

"Wisdom can be a burden sometimes. Mr. Baldini, you really shouldn't smoke those." Then he smiles and puts it back in his pocket. "Let us set up Luca Junior's treatment schedule, when can you fly him in?"

By the end of the meeting with Baldini, I'd arranged for his son to be treated, for Avery to be set free of his threats and for Harmon to meet an untimely end. I wanted to let her know I was coming for her, that this time I would save her and not just from herself but from all of this. I let some of her voicemails play in the car as I drive out to the estate, she sounded so broken her voice quivered with tears that I couldn't see, but I felt every single one. I was going to fix this, all of it. I thought I could let go, move on and forget, but the heart will never forget its first love. Eiran was hers, she will always have the shadow of that love cast over her and that shadow only makes me love her more. I park my car at the visitors centre of the wine farm where tourists come to taste the wines made here and walk through the vineyards up to her home. After passing the small cemetery, I stop for a minute near a burnt out tree to contemplate just how much she's lost and how little she had to lose. These are all the people she had, there's no one left to love her. I want to succeed where they failed. I want to love her more than anything in the world. My feet crunch on the small stones in the pathway that winds up the hill and comes up behind the house right near the window to her room. The memories of us in that bed make my heart beat faster, the image of her half-painted half-pure body tied up for my pleasure has me already salivating. The leaves on the vines are rustling in the wind that is blowing down the hill, the sound is almost a roar as so many leaves move all at once. Pushing past the low branches of the last vines beside the house, I'm stopped dead by the vision in front of me, she's there on her bed, the curtains are wide open. The afternoon sun is highlighting her inked flesh as she moves. It's not the living work of art that has me stopped, but the sight of her moving that way with him. She rides him with flowing movements as he just lays there taking what she has to give. The way her breasts bounce and her nails dig into his chest, I want to run away but I can't stop watching. The jealousy is soon replaced by the sadness of loss and I leave them. I can't watch her being with him, he is the one I'm supposed to save her from. I close my eyes and walk back down the path, nothing could hurt me like what I have just seen. There's a reason I never stayed anywhere, why I didn't allow myself to love, I was protecting myself from the agony of loss. When I reach the graves, I walk to the far edge where the fallen stump of the burnt tree lies. I sit on it and my eyes catch the chains that must have held up a swing, a swing that she would have used. She watched her father mourn for years, now I sit here in the same spot and I mourn the loss of a love I never had the chance to live. I chastise myself for being so stupid to think that I had truly changed her, that the murderer could be a lover. Of all people in this world, I should have known better than this. I let my heart guide me and it steered me off a cliff and into a fire pit. Burying my head in my hands, I let my broken heart escape in tears. I purge the pain, not even the slice of her beloved blade could cut this deep into my soul. I almost wish she had just killed me that first night, then I knew I was courting the devil, now I know she is so much more than death.

I sit there among the dead, haunted by so many things. Callum's buried right there. I helped him die, I listened to his crazy stories including his warped dream of her and Harmon being together and creating this invincible crime family. I wish I had told him it was time before Harmon arrived, that I had told her what was going on. The threats to my life and my mercy mission filled me with fear that overrode my desire for her, my logic muffled the screams in my heart and I left. I ran. I abandoned her to the wolves that were there only to eat her.

The sun is sinking in the sky and in the milky pre-dusk light the noise of the leaves is replaced with an eerie silence as the wind dies down. I watch the shadows of the graves move with the fading light when my silent refection is slashed by the loud barks of a dog I know too well, before I get the chance to look around Jameson has pounced on me, licking and pawing and making sounds that resemble more cat than dog. He whines and wags his silly tail that fast he might put his back out.

"Shh, hey boy, I missed you too." I pet him and rub his ears and even embrace the dog I hadn't realised I missed so much. "Jameson, down boy." I try to calm him before he alerts the whole farm to my presence. He calms down to a mild panic and sits next to me his whole body still vibrates with his tail wagging and his butt doesn't actually touch the floor. I smile at the joy the canine brings wherever he goes. When I helped his owner leave the world behind I had no idea I would make a friend like him. Distracted by the fur ball and his affections my sadness was momentarily forgotten, but it collided with me full force when I heard her voice.

"Jameson what are you . . . it's you. Mathew?" A smile lights her face and she throws her arms around me as if she was not just with another man. "God I have missed you." Tears from her eyes wet my shirt as she cries. I don't hold her yet she claws onto me as if I am the only thing keeping her alive. "You can stop lying, Avery. I saw you." I push her away from me, feeling her is not helping me forget what I witnessed earlier. She looks down at the floor her lip trembles and tears stain her face. "You broke all the rules." I step back a little forcing space between us.

"You left," she stammers, stepping closer again.

"I had to leave, but you know that. I came back, I fixed things so that you could be free of it all, free of that world and I walk in to find you in the bed that we shared, with him. Of all people, the one I warned you about, he's the one you chose to replace me with." I'm yelling at her and she cowers away from me, her mind still trained to expect punishment for breaking rules. "I fucking loved you enough to come back!" I turn and walk away leaving her and our damn dog standing with the dead bodies that seem to surround her, I should have torn my heart out and buried it there with them. Jameson the traitor sits beside her where I can see the sobs shaking her body, as I glance back she crumples to the floor beside him and he looks at me like I stole his ball. My steps slow down, but I'm still walking away.

"Stop! Stop! You can't leave me again." I hear her yell and I freeze, I can't look back again, I just stand there frozen on the spot. The thud of indecision pounds with my heartbeat, my brain says just go, leave it all behind and go far away from here. My heart is aching to hold her in my arms again, but her betrayal has wounded me and the fear of more pain halts me. Her footsteps on the gravel path crunch and grind as she gets closer. "You think you know what you saw, you think I broke the rules, but you have no idea the hell I'm living right now. I broke the rules because you said I would know when to fight and for now this is the only way to fight him." She slaps me hard on my back it stings me even through my shirt. "Look at me dammit, I phoned, I left messages. I told you I needed you and you never came so I had no choice." Slap another stinging blow. "Look at me, you didn't even bother to tell me your name. How can you be angry I don't even know who you are?" I catch her wrist before the next blow lands, rage is coursing through me and I want to hurt her the way she has hurt me. "You know me more than anyone else ever has, Avery. My name is inconsequential, it's just a name. I suggest you start explaining to me how fucking Harmon is fighting, because I am seconds away from leaving the carnage that is your life for good. Some people are just not worth saving." She sucks in a startled sob as my words cut like her knife, I get a strange satisfaction out of that split second of pain. I point to the graves behind us. "Every person that gets near to you or your family dies, I'm the angel of death. I know what it is like to carry death wherever I go, I don't need to come home to it. I watch people in excruciating pain all day, I don't want to come home and feel the agony of hurt caused by the person I love. I don't want this life, Avery and if you do then I can't have you." My voice sounds deeper as it soaks with anger and honest truth. I don't want this world, I want no part of this place or the life she has here. If she cannot leave every last bit of it behind her then she can't be in my future.

"I needed him to think I was willing to have his kid, the one his brother had concocted as a plan to tie us together. I had a plan I just needed him to think I was trying until his time runs out. I didn't want Amya to be pulled into this, to be forced into bloodying her hands in this company. I am trying to find a better way." The tears roll down her cheeks and fall to the dusty floor at her feet. She sniffs and wipes her nose with the back of her hand. "I was trying so hard to be selfless." She collapses on the floor next to Jameson, as broken as the day I first saw her yet healed in so many ways.

"Get up, Avery." I reach out my hand to her and Jameson snarls and snaps at me, like he is protecting her from me, as if I would hurt her right now. I couldn't even if I tried, she's so defeated in her own turmoil nothing I did would even be felt. "Is he still up there?" I ask her as she stumbles to her feet without taking my hand. She shakes her head looking at the floor between us. "Let's go and have a talk." I put my arm around her and it instantly feel like I have found home again, like I belong right in that small space beside her. "I cannot believe you actually came back," she whispers the words as our dog darts between our legs running circles around us and barking like a fool.

The house has not changed at all, the door at the end of the passage to her father's room is still closed and nothing has been added or taken away bar the picture she had of Callum and her on the mantle. Everyone else is still there but his image is conspicuously missing from the line. We both just stand in the space between the lounge and the kitchen, I'm looking at her and maybe seeing clearly for the first time and her odd eyes are looking at me with emotion that's been missing for so long from her. I hand her my phone. "You need to call Amya, we all need to sit down and have a very honest talk. Because, Avery this plan is stupid. He's going to get desperate as the time starts to run out and I do not trust that he won't do something that could put you and your life in danger. The man is not all there."

She pulls her phone out and searches for the number, I know he will have her phone calls watched that's why I said she should use mine.

"Amya? It's me, are you in the city?" Her eyes find mine as she speaks to the one person in all of this who seems to have escaped the insanity and carnage.

"Please can you come to the farm, I need to talk to you." She can't stand still and shifts from one leg to the other. "Yes, now if you can."

When she ends the call I take her hand and we sit down in the lounge, I sit next to her needing that feeling that I get when she's near to me. "I can fix this whole thing for you, I have spoken with Bladini. He will compromise on some things if we can get Amya to help us you and I can walk away leave this place and start over." She looks at me as if I am the superhero that flew in with a cape and rescued her from some monster.

AMYA HAS AN AIR of peace about her, she's different, there is still a definite darkness in her, but she is a beautiful woman that doesn't exude the same evil that everyone else in this family did. Avery seems intimidated by her, the dynamics between women are always somewhat strange to me, a room full of men is so much easier than two women. Robin is with her, I haven't met either of them before only through Callum's stories and what I saw at his funeral. She looks like a pin-up girl, almost animated she is so perfect and he is huge hulking man that towers over, even me. I recognise the tell-tale gang tattoo on his face, this man is from the toughest streets in the city and has lived to walk away from them.

Avery embraces her and silent tears start to fall again, Amya wipes them away like a mother would and kisses her forehead. "This is, umm, this is Mathew." She steps aside and introduces us I shake hands with them both, Robin grips my hand very tightly a silent threat. They are both older than us, but not as old as Callum and Rowan were I put her in her fifties. "Hi, Mathew." Amya greets softly as we walk inside to the lounge area, she passes us and opens the patio doors wide. "Let's sit outside, Avery."

The sun has set and the night air is cooler, we all settle around the large wooden table. Robin goes back in and returns with two bottles of wine and glasses from the kitchen, as if he has lived here before. I feel like the outsider in this situation. I wonder if I will ever be a part of her life, I want to be in all aspects of her life. I blink my eyes closed and pinch the bridge of my nose as my mind is filled with the images of her and Harmon from earlier and I fight the need to puke. Forgiving her is not going to be easy and I am not sure I want to, I don't think us is an option any longer. I can't see her leaving all of this behind, even if she does it will follow her, it's in her blood. She was born to be the queen of this kingdom, and as much as it pains me I almost see rational in Callum's sick plan. They would make the most formidable criminal team in history, maybe I shouldn't have stepped in, maybe he did know what was best.

Shaking off the insane thoughts that are permeating my brain, I look up to see her looking at me, begging me with her eyes to just give her an answer. I don't have one to give, my heart is undecided about her now. I shake my head and look away.

"What's going on, Avery?" Amya urges her to start talking. She looks concerned.

"I tried. I did. I just can't." Avery stammers back, her eyes on me as she tries to tell them that she is going to essentially throw them under the bus to get out of this mess.

"You can't what?" I detect some annoyance in Amya's voice. "This is not my mess, Avery. I walked away from my family twenty-odd years ago for a reason. I'm not a part of anything my stupid brothers concocted. I have helped you where I can." She is scolding her like a child and it gets my hackles up.

"Amya, if I may. I have met with Baldini, I'm helping him so to say. He's willing to take O'Reilly International off of you directly. This would allow Avery to get rid of Harmon and be free of all this, just like you are." She looks at me considering what I have said, but I see the darkness and anger bubbling up inside her.

"You want me to give the family business to the brother of the man that destroyed our lives, then you want me to be okay with her killing my only living relative so she can be free of something that was born into her." She reaches out to Avery's shirt and exposes the huge black heart on her chest and then shows the same thing on hers, "Mathew, you know how I know she will never be free. You know who told here about black hole children when she was an infant with no mother? There is no freedom for us." She just reiterates what I had feared, this cycle cannot be broken.

"So, in short no. I helped her put together a plan that secures the company for the Italian without it ever having to be mine at all. As for killing my brother, Avery killed every other person she took to bed directly or indirectly so I don't see how he, or you will escape her demons alive." The bitterness in this woman now almost has me speechless. She will never help, I was wrong to think she was on Avery's side and that she cared. She cannot care because just like Rowan, Callum and everyone else in this family she has no feelings.

I watch as Avery tries to keep her crying quiet in the corner, I look at her and I wish I had the same hope I saw before. I don't think it's worth saving her, this is her, she's like them.

She turns to Avery, her eyes are filled with anger and bitter rage. "I told you young lady, this is not my problem and I refuse to be the solution. I helped you. Suck it up and deal with Harmon. It's another nine months, it won't fucking kill you." She pushes her chair back and stands up, shooting Robin a glare, I have never met such a silent man. Not a word comes out of his mouth. As she walks away from the table, he looks at Avery where she sits defeated and falling to pieces and he shakes his head, he is sorry for her. Not sorry enough to say anything though. As Amya stomps off to the front door Robin rounds the table and bends down to where my love is broken, he puts an arm around her shoulder and leans against her, like he loved her once. "Kill the bastard. I will deal with the wrath of Amya. You go be free, you deserve it and I know your mother would not have wanted this for you. I helped her forget her pain and I'm telling you, let go of yours and forget about my wife. She is bitter, angry and life was cruel to her." He kisses the top of her head, stands and reaches over to shake my hand offering me a nod before he follows his wife out of the house.

I love Avery but I am not sure the love of one person can save someone who has no other love in their life, I worry that loving her will destroy me and that there will be nothing left of either of us. I should never have come back to this place the day of that funeral. I made a terrible mistake loving her.

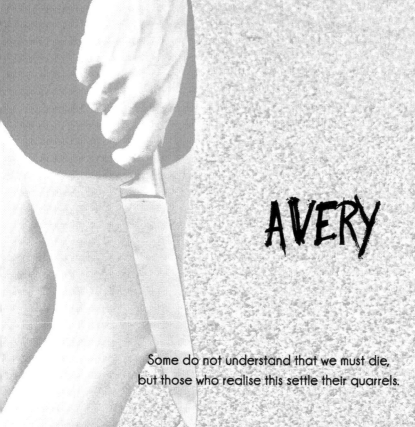

AVERY

Some do not understand that we must die,
but those who realise this settle their quarrels.

CHOICES. SOMETHING I never considered before in my life. I made them without considering consequence. I did whatever I wanted and never looked back, I never allowed myself to feel the pain of the things I did. Then he came and made me understand that my actions affected everyone and while I could switch the feelings off the other people that my knife sliced through were not spared the agony. Now I need saving from the pain, I need to be considered and Amya just walked away and left me with the choice, if I do what I need to save myself then I will hurt her. Her actions have shown me that in this world no one cares about my feelings they simply expect me not to have any. My heart is shredded and I feel that even though he left, Mathew was mine until today, when he saw me with Harmon I broke the thread that tied us together. Now I need to choose, if I choose him and kill Harmon, I leave everything that ties me to my family behind and there's a chance that he will still be gone because I hurt him. If I set him free, then I choose Harmon. Then I need to embrace the idea that Callum had in his sick mind that this family needed to be joined and an heir to carry on the future of our madness was the way. I need to stop dreaming of killing the idiot and try to feel something other than loathing for him, I would have to seek out the connection that he has already created in his sick mind. Maybe monsters belong with monsters and I should just tell Mathew to stay away before I destroy him too, I will kill him slowly or swiftly being near me is a death sentence.

He left me sitting here to consider things hours ago, only now I wish I had tried to stop him.

"You need to decide and so do I, Avery. I can't promise you that I will come back. I'm afraid to love you because you have already hurt me and I cannot stay to be destroyed by toxic love. Think about your life, you need to follow that heart. You told me you were a black hole, well you sucked me in, consumed me and made me lose myself in you now I need to try and fix that. Bye, my angel." He kissed my lips softly and left. The electric spark of our past kisses absent now.

The house is empty and dark, I haven't bothered with lights. I just sit in the blackness and consider how true it is. My father once said to me that he would rather raise me to be a monster than allow the monsters to eat me alive. I was too young then to understand what he meant, but as I sit next to his blood stain on the bed I think I finally get it now. I was waiting for a saviour, waiting for Mathew to fix me, fix my life when I am the only person who has that power. No one can save me except myself. In making me the villain my father left me open to be eaten alive by my own monsters, he failed me in so many ways. I lie in the spot where he died because Harmon lied, we all know that Callum murdered Renzo, it was like a campfire story to us all. He was the big bad wolf and Callum was the unsung hero that came and killed him, it was meant to set my father free but nothing could break the bond he had with my mother. When I think about it they were straight out of a Shakespeare novel, his love stories were labeled tragedies for a reason, because real love destroys you.

Now I'm here, alone and there's nothing but silence surrounding me. Silence and the sadness that when I needed them most, my family was gone and I was left behind. My mother's letters spoke of following my heart and finding my place in the world, I don't think I have one. Jameson nudges me with his wet nose, he is also sad that Mathew left again. He whines a little and I realise I haven't fed the poor dog yet and it's way most past his dinner time. Sliding off the end of the bed, I walk through the dark house to the kitchen, I drop his metal bowl and the clang echo in the emptiness. Flicking on a light as I got to the pantry to get his food out, the empty kitchen glows and my eyes adjust to the light.

"Here you go, silly boy." I pet Jameson's head as he patiently sits for his dinner, he's now the one constant in my life. There when I wake and there when I sleep every single day. No person has ever had that presence in my life and the true solitude of my existence surrounds me. I'm always going to be alone.

I STROLL BACK DOWN to the graveyard just before dawn, I miss the swing and the tree from when I was young. I miss sitting here watching my dad cry for her. Now the row of headstones has gotten longer, Mick, my Mom, Eiran and Callum are all here. A nauseating anger turns my stomach as I look at them all resting peacefully in a line while I struggle with the torment they all left behind. I stand over Callum and I cannot help but scream at him.

"I idolised you, I trusted you, I did everything in this fucking world to please you and for what? You lied! You used me!" I spit on his grave the fury in me escaping now. "You never cared further than some sick plan you had conjured up in your demented mind. No wonder she killed you! I want to kill you only you are already dead. I hate you now, I hope you know that. I fucking hate you."

I rest against his headstone so he can hear this bit clearly. "I'm going to destroy your little empire, Callum, I'm going to give it away. I don't want to be the queen and your brother will be the last prince in your fairytale because I am going to gut him." The words are a whispered hiss before I stand and move to Eiran.

"You shouldn't be here, but I loved you despite the monster you were. I let you take from me and I took from you. So this grave is our truce." His grave is not elaborate it has only his first name on it. I kiss my hand and touch the top of it as I walk over to where my parents are buried beside one another.

I cannot find words for them, so I sit between them and cry. I cry for the mom I never had and the father that was lost to grief before he could love me. I cry because I'm a killer and because I know that will always be inside me. The sobbing doesn't stop, every heartache and fear I was never allowed to feel is coming to live in between them and I'm letting it all go so that I can be free. Next time I visit this place, I want it to be with a peaceful heart, I don't want to come here hating them again. When the sun appears over the hilltop I get up and dust the sand off my pants, Jameson is at my heels waiting to follow me wherever I go. I love waking the path through the vines to the house, it's like an enchanted world where nothing else exists for the time you are in there. I pick a grape and bite it, but spit the sour globe back out. Thankfully our wines taste better than the grapes that was awful. Jameson is quick to lick it up, he has no tastebuds at all. When I open the gate to the house, I'm met with Harmon leaning on his car nattering to someone on the phone. His face is pulled tight with agitation and he glares at me like I just killed his kitten. That glare just made my choices that much easier. I ignore him and unlock the front door allowing Jameson to barrel in without knocking me off my feet before I walk inside my home. Harmon isn't far behind me still whining on the phone to someone, I go to the kitchen and put the coffee machine on.

"Where the fuck have you been? I have been calling you half the damn night woman?" He booms at me as he hangs up his phone call. "There was shit to deal with, Avery. People get pissed when you aren't available."

"People, or you, Harmon? I was busy, I had things to deal with that were my business and not yours." I seethe back at him. "Well it is still my four days of the month so since I thought you were dead and I drove all this damn way let's fuck then I'll drive us to work." It is like a gunshot goes off inside my head, the noise of his intrusion on my life is deafening, blinding and drives me to the pinnacle of my own madness. There was a good reason the O'Reilly family was all dead, they are a plague and I am going to eradicate them. I stand dead still with my coffee in my hand and just look at him, he is perfect on the outside the ideal trap for anyone who gets close. He would make a handsome husband and I bet his babies would be pretty if I let him live to have any, but I won't. I'm not fooled by conventional beauty, nor am I lured by money. I have my own money and I do not need a man. My life is testament to succeeding alone, I have learned a lesson from Callum and Shannon—two monsters cannot be together. My parents taught me the same lesson, it is impossible for them not to destroy each other. I will not be destroyed for this dick, when I let love destroy me it will be with someone worth spilling my blood for, because love is sacrifice. I was never going to love this man, we were a nuclear explosion waiting to happen.

"Go to my room, I'm coming, Harmon." I send him away so I can find what I need in the office. "I just want to drink my coffee and put the dog out so I don't have to listen to him barking at your naked ass." My dog hates him, always trust your dog they have great sense about these things.

Harmon sulks off down the passage and I open the kitchen door for Jameson on the way to the office, as much I want to slice the flesh from his bones and make him suffer I don't have the time, he will know the second he sees me that I'm going to kill him, I won't be able to hide my intentions for long. The familiar feeling that claws its way up my spine as I anticipate the moment I put an end to all of this mayhem, the second I kill him, I'll crave the rush this time. This time I want to kill so badly it hurts me, I imagine my knife slicing into his flesh, staining that perfect skin with his blood. Tearing his beautiful, deceitful muscles from his bones, running my blade from his sternum to crotch. Killing him slowly would be so satisfying, instead I will have to settle for a single bullet from the gun next to my bed. Quick and relatively painless which is so much more than he deserves, running my finger along the blade of my favourite knife. The razor sharp stainless steel taunts me with possibilities. I pick it up and grab some cable ties with it, I might be able to have some fun with this yet. I lose the ability to control this desire for blood and death.

"Are you coming, Avery? We have to get to the office at some point too," he yells at me from the room down the passage. I grind my teeth and close the door behind me as I imagine what comes next. The good part and the part where I have to get close to him. I swallow the rising bile in my throat as I step into the doorway he is already half undressed. If I didn't know who or what he was I would look at his bare chest and bite my bottom lip, instead, I struggle to contain my gag reflex and rage. He watches me as I look at him, he thinks I'm admiring the view, his cocky smile is taunting my demons to play. I'm looking but I'm not admiring in the way he thinks. I'm imagining the way my knife will carve through those abdominal muscles. Crimson blood pouring from him and pooling around his lifeless, waste of a body. The pictures in my head are vile, I shouldn't want to kill someone so badly, I have killed many before but this desire hasn't accompanied those kills. I lust for his death.

"Take off your pants and lie down Harmon. I want to have some fun today. This baby making shit is getting tedious," I say, side stepping so he cannot see me lay my knife on the dresser. He shoves his pants down and folds them, this man's control issues are off the charts. I watch him settle himself on my bed, his hands behind his head and the arrogance bleeding from him. It's almost too perfect, too easy as I straddle him with the cable ties held in my teeth, he looks at me with greedy lust on those stupid eyes. Sliding my hands under his head, I bind his hands together right where they are. His eyes get big and he lets out a growl from his throat as I lean down and kiss him, a kiss of death. Sliding down the length of his naked body I slip off the end of the bed and stand there. I look over every inch of my enemy and I feel the betrayal of his brother, the man I admired. The person whose approval I sought every day for most of my life. I offered him my kidney, I would have died to save him and it was all a lie. A carefully crafted plan to get me to give him what he wanted most and couldn't buy. The violent malice of his forward planning have set the killer in me completely free, there is no consequence for this action. Anyone who feels sorry, sad or hurt by this murder deserves to feel the torment.

I slide out of my clothes, it's easier to clean myself up afterwards that way. Harmon licks his lips and rakes over me with eyes, he is partially restrained but I will still have to move quickly so he can't hurt me or get away. I grab his tie and bind one leg to my bedpost, he thinks I'm being kinky. It's turning him on and his hard cock is on display in the bright morning light. The sun catches the ridges of his perfectly sculpted and manicured body, I wonder how much he spends on waxing? I turn my back, draw in a cleansing breath and grab my knife off the dresser, it fits perfectly in my fist allowing me to wield it with power and finesse.

"Let's play a game, Harmon." I turn around and bring the blade to my mouth, biting down on the sharp end strolling back to him I see his eyes grow wide. He doesn't know if I'm actually playing a game or not. Picking up my undies off the floor I crumple them into a ball and as I clamber back over his naked body avoiding his dick. I shove them in his mouth that was gaping open with shock. Silenced, bound and vulnerable, I see the fear creeping over him, his cock turns flaccid. He squirms beneath me but I have him pinned with my whole body weight.

"Do you want a baby, Harmon?" I whisper in his ear. "I don't want babies, they would end up like us. Fucked up monsters with nothing to lose." I sit and watch his eyes as he closes them and opens again in the hope he is dreaming this. "You see, Harmon, if you don't feel anything, if you are not attached to anything you cannot suffer. You can't lose anything you don't have. A child would be an attachment. Something I could lose. Something that could hurt me. Because I would love it. Love is the most excruciatingly painful thing in this world. So we are not having any babies. In fact we no longer exist. I'm taking back my life, your brother fucking stole my childhood, every action has a consequence this is the consequence of his." My knife plummets into his chest with force, the sound of it hitting bone and tearing flesh is cathartic, a high like no other surges through me as I pull it free and watch his tears flow. His head shakes violently from side to side begging me through the gag in his mouth. I cannot stop, I'm setting myself free and nothing will stop me now. His blood stains my hands and sticks to my body as I mutilate the flesh and blood of my childhood tormentor. I never considered how Callum had tormented me into being the little girl he needed and not the girl I was born to be. This is me! The killer not the queen of his depraved empire, I'm not meant to sell people or diamonds. I never wanted to trade in human spare parts or ammunitions to start wars. He stole me from who I am and now his stupid brother is paying the price for it.

Wiping my hair out of my face and smearing what's left of him on my skin, I stand up on the bed ready to step off, the carnage is beautiful as I see the blood pool on my bed. I smile and for the very first time I know exactly who I am. When I look up out the window my attention drawn to Jameson barking, I see Mathew standing at the gate watching me. I can see his heart breaking from here as my demons have shown their true colours. Naked, covered in blood and completely exposed, I cannot hide any part of myself from him like this. If he can love me through this then his love is real and if he leaves me now, I know my monsters are bigger than the angel in him. He may be an angel of death but to me he was a saviour, a guardian angel. To me, he was love.

I close my eyes to stop the tears that threaten to fall and when I open them, he's gone, the gate is open and him and my dog are gone. I'm alone again. I'm always alone.

NOT MATTHEW

Grief is the price of love.

ONCE MY MIND HAS reconciled the fact that while she was with Harmon physically, she never gave him her heart, she didn't let him in and for her the physical was meaningless. She had given me her heart, bruised, battered and bloody but it was still beating for me, I can't ignore what she does to me or how I'm drawn to her, even the darkness in her pulls me closer. I drown my irrational jealousy in a bottle of liquor, it isn't even good booze it just numbs out the pain and quiets the screaming voices telling me to leave and never look back. I saved her, at least I did everything I could to save her. If she doesn't want to be saved that is not on me. By the time the sun and my phone wake me from my self-inflicted coma, it's mid-morning. My head is pounding like a snare drum and my mouth is dry with the vile after effects of my wallowing. Showering the hangover away as much as I can and drown the rest in black coffee strong enough to fuel a car. One thing is still there in my thumping head. Her.

I know I said I had to think and that she had to decide but that was my ego talking and I need to go back there and tell her that I understand. I need to help her choose right. I want her to choose me even if I am not sure that I have chosen her. I'm selfish. But I know that being with her will hurt me, ruin me and change me forever and I am not ready to change.

I drive the long commute to her as fast as I can, not wanting the haze of my hangover to dissipate and allow me to think clearly. I don't have the code to get in the residential gates so I park at the farm entrance and walk through the vineyard past the cemetery and up the hill to house. I can feel the sweat of last night's drinking and the sun beating down on me as it coats my skin and makes my clothing stick to me. I'm not dressed for hiking in the heat of the mid-morning sun and I shove my sleeves up as high as the will go. Jameson finds me half way up the hill his wagging tail as he runs in circles around me whips against my legs and I try to pet him but he is moving too fast. "Come on boy. Calm down I want to get up there." I talk to the silly dog in an attempt to get him from under my feet.

As I reach the threshold where I was assaulted by her betrayal yesterday, I'm again met with an image I cannot ever wipe from my mind. I watch, frozen as she cuts him up, ripping his flesh apart with a knife. Her naked body painted in blood red murder, I knew he had to die. God I have killed people, but this is savage. My eyes won't look away, the angel I love is replaced by a monster that I never dreamed existed in her. I must be a fool, I knew there were over eighty men missing, dead and disposed of by her hand. I was cocky enough to believe that I was different, that I could tame the beast inside her. A part of me is dying with him, the hope I had clung to all my life is being brutally slaughtered with every stab of her blade into his flesh. Avery was without a doubt born to be a killer, she murders him with grace and carnal beauty and takes me right along with him. I can almost feel the physical pain of every puncture and slice as it carves through the flesh of my love for her. I don't love this savage villain that I see now. Who could love that?

My affections are turned to stone and dust as she stands behind the glass and our eyes meet, those viciously contrasted eyes bore into my soul and pull my heart out. I want to hold her and heal this gaping wound in me but I know that this is not an illusion this is her truth. I cannot save her because she isn't real. The calm part of me wants to walk away and not glance back instead the anger makes me go inside. I need the closure of seeing all of her up close, stripped bare and right in front of my eyes, my blindness needs to be cured. I had wanted to kill him, my way would have had the same end result but it would have been clinical, detached and peaceful. I see death as an end to suffering, she made him suffer, pulled the pain from his body with each slash. Dragging his torture out so that she could feast on his agony. She was enjoying it, I have seen that look in her eyes. The same pleasure she expressed as I made love to her. I was fucking a monster all this time only now I see her clearly.

My legs carry me down the passage to the bed where we slept and he died, the place where my heart felt full and I had found home. To her, and the shattered remains of my love. Her back is to me and she's still staring out of the window to where I was watching, the knife dangles at her side in a lose grip while it drips blood to a small pool on the floor. Even in that state she is a sight to behold, even in her depraved honest darkness she is stunning.

"What have you done, Avery?" I whisper as my eyes are met with the carnage on the bed. Blood and body parts are blended into a red blur there is very little left of him at all.

"What I was born to do." She hangs her head and answers me with little conviction. I believe her.

"Why, my angel? Why?" I try to take in the scene inside the room but my mind doesn't want to accept it.

"Just go, Mathew. I already know you are going to leave, you told me from the very beginning that you were not in my life to stay. No one is meant to stay in my life, I can only lose what I cling to right. Well I'm letting you go so I can't lose you. Just fucking go, Mathew! I need to get this cleaned." When she turns to face me and I see her red teary eyes I want to go to her, but I stand still frozen by the truth. "Leave!" she screams now, moving towards me, she is tightening her grip on that knife and without thinking I run.

Fight or flight. I flew. I flew away from the black hole before I was gone forever. I am honouring my promise to Baldini and treating his son, but I want nothing else from these people or the parallel universe in which they exist. I want to forget I ever answered Callum's emails and that I hadn't been brought to them at all. I don't regret loving Avery but I want to forget the pain that it caused me. I was warned, more than once that she would kill me, while my heart still beats and my lungs still fill with air she succeeded. I'm dead inside.

AVERY

The world is filled with death and decay. But the wise do not grieve, having realised the nature of the world.

HARMON IS DEAD.
Mathew is gone.
I'm alone. Again.

As his blood dries on my skin turning sticky and thick, I'm still frozen, standing in the hell I created. The scarlet masterpiece painted around me is a reminder of what I truly am. I have embraced the darkness inside, let it come out to play in the light and the freedom is exhilarating. I said I had two faces, well I am choosing to wear this one. Walking into the small guest bathroom across the passage to shower the remnants of Harmon off of myself, I feel a tranquility in me that has been missing since I was four. The last time I felt this way was before I saw the photos of Renzo Baldini's dead body on my mother's grave, before I knew I was meant to kill. I was just a little girl with pig tails and funny eyes. Before Callum. The quiet truth of my life settles into me as I wash the matted bits of my hair and clean my skin. Scrubbing my fingers until they are raw to make sure there is no evidence. Dressing myself as if I'm going to work like any other day, I pin my hair up and put my make up on. Harmon's remains are reflected in the mirror behind me making me smile as I slide my lipstick on. I wipe my front teeth to make sure there are no red smudges and I pick up my phone from next to the bed, I have some calls to make.

Dialing the men that my father used for his cleanups, not the O'Reilly crew, as I walk down the hall to go and get another coffee from the machine in the kitchen.

"Hello, it's Avery," I say as the line picks up.

"Address, body count and special instructions ma'am?" The husky voice asks me like this was nothing out of the ordinary at all.

"My home, one and feed him to the crocodiles. You will need to dispose of the bed, bedroom furniture and wood flooring too. Sorry I have made an awful mess." I apologise when I am not even a little sorry.

"Yes, ma'am. It's good to have you back on our team if I may say so." The friendly tone of his voice makes this all feel so perfectly right.

"Thank you. We can meet tomorrow and discuss the future but today I have other messes to clean up myself."

"Good day, ma'am, leave it with us." The line goes dead and I make the next call, one I know will be a little harder to navigate. I need a death certificate for that idiot so that the company can be tied up and handed off to Amya and Baldini. My friend the chief of police will give it to me, but it's going to cost me a lot. His phone rings for ages before he answers.

"Hello, Avery, to what do I owe the honour of a personal call?" Thuli answers the call with way too much energy.

"Thuli, always so full of it. I need a death certificate, a no questions asked, there is no body, just a death certificate my friend. Can you make that happen for me?" He is silent for a second or two.

"Hmm, it depends is anyone going to miss this body that doesn't exist?" He doesn't want any backlash, typical government employee.

"No one but me, just tell me how much it will cost and I will transfer the funds Thuli. We both know you can." I don't really have time to sit here and bargain with the man.

"Fine, but I want a hundred grand. Send me the details. Avery, how come this one needs a note? The others they just go away. Why's he different?" Nosy bastard.

"Because he's Harmon O'Reilly. That's why." I clarify the situation for him, we pay this man a shit ton of money to stay stupid, he had best keep it up or he'll be the next one needing a death certificate.

"Eish, you don't play nice with others do you?" The way his sounds whistle through his teeth makes my skin crawl.

"Bye, Thuli, just get it done and I will send you the money." There is no one in this country that is incorruptible, they all have a price and O'Reilly International has been paying most of them for years. I grab my travel mug and keys before looking around for Jameson. I walk outside and call for him. "Jameson, come boy lets go." He loves a car ride and if king dick isn't at work, I'm taking my dog with me. I don't want him here while they are busy cleaning up, he scrambles back up the hill through the open gate that Mathew must have left through. My heart sinks a little but I know making him leave was right, saving him from me was the best thing I could do for him and the hardest thing I could do for me. He wouldn't be able to love me past what he witnessed and I know now without a doubt that I am looking for love, untainted love. A love that won't ask where I've come from and what I have done, a love that wouldn't care if they knew. Mathew cares, he feels things so deeply and watching me this morning has wounded his soul in way I know will never heal right. I slide into the seat of the Mercedes I bought to replace the Jag. It's sleek, silver and inconspicuous but fast as all hell. Callum may have been right about cars all along, but I wouldn't admit that to him, living or dead. The drive to the city puts a distance between me and my actions, it's well after lunch before I step out of the lift into the reception area of our offices, waiting for me is the elderly Italian. His face is wrinkled with years of frowning and he walks with a cane, he stands taking giant effort to heave himself up off the chair and smiles at me.

"Mr. Baldini, what a pleasant surprise." I grit out through my clenched teeth, he got here fast. I know he has people watching me, but this is getting a bit much. Jameson is darting about sniffing everything and everyone in the place.

"You don't have to pretend, no one's ever happy to see me, not even my own children like it when I visit." He holds out a hand to shake mine and I oblige. I'm not sure yet what to make of this man, but he has given me a way out and I'm thankful for that if nothing else in this world. I should hate him for killing my father, but I don't. For some reason I know he was manipulated into it by Harmon. I also know my dad wasn't really living, he wouldn't have been sad to die.

"People call you the Wrath behind your back, I don't know maybe you should smile occasionally?" I jest with him as we walk to my office down the short passage. He really is a grumpy old man.

We sit in my reclaimed office and Jameson finds a spot to lie under my desk, he loves coming to the office, all the attention and treats.

"So, why did you choose to come back now, I can't believe it took twenty years for you to find us." I raise an eyebrow, because I really do want to know what sparked his sudden interest in coming here. He crosses his legs and leans back in the chair making himself comfortable in what will ultimately be his office soon.

"Before now, I was busy, I had a wife, my business and my children to occupy my time. Now my wife is dead and eldest son is dying, I decided it was time I found closure. I never truly grieved for my brother and grief is the price of love. It was just time, I didn't want to die angry." He sounds sad when he lists the people he has lost like that, it's echoed in his dull eyes that mist with tears never cried.

"Your brother didn't deserve your grief, or your love." I let my anger towards the man that murdered my mother show.

"Renzo was only my half-brother, he was eight years older than me. I loved him, admired him, wanted to be him and I never stood up for him I was a cowardly boy, and an even more cowardly man." His posture changes and he seems embarrassed about the way he treated his brother.

"And he was a monster that didn't deserve your affections." I sit down now, I don't like talking about him or my mother. "He tortured my mother, killed her spirit, murdered her children and when that wasn't enough he took her, with a bullet. A cowardly gun shot. He was the coward, not you. So far I have seen you are not like him at all and that's a good thing." He shakes his head and moves forward so his eyes bore into mine.

"What do you know, Avery, you were a baby in your cot. What do you really know about your mother and her family, do you know where your grandmother came from?" He asks questions that sting because I know nothing. I was only ever told the stories they wanted me to hear, the ones that would turn me cold and make me a better heir to this business. That was Callum's doing once again.

"Not much at all really, I know that my grandfather Mick is buried at the estate and that my grandmother left when Lauri was a toddler, Mick came here to keep them safe from Callum's family." I stutter out the little history I do know.

"Secrets they are mistaken for lies. My father hated Renzo, loathed the air that boy breathed. He beat him and tortured him, burned him with his cigars so that the smell would fill the house and Renzo's screams would rattle the glass. This went on for years, even when Renzo was older and strong enough to fight back, it continued. One day my brother woke up and learned some truths that had been kept from him. He walked into our father's office and killed him, then he went to find your mother." He sighs and wrings his hands together on top of his cane. "Their marriage was not love, or fate or a fairy tale. It was pure revenge, my brother hunted her down and destroyed her with purpose." I know this part of the story, Mick had killed his mother and unborn brother.

"Because Mick had murdered his mother, I know that." Laughter cackles from him and he shakes his head at me again, it isn't funny. My mother didn't deserve to pay for Mick's sins. It makes me think for a minute. Indirectly am I paying for Rowan's sins? Did my father's actions result in my unhappiness?

"Oh yes, Mick killed Renzo's mother, but my sweet child, it was revenge for so much more than that. Your mother and Renzo, they shared so much more than the world knew about. It took me years to work it all out clearly and put the puzzle together. My Nonna eventually told me the whole story in pieces through her dementia."

"They shared nothing! He was a living breathing fucking devil! She was destroyed by him and his evil soul. I am sorry but *my daddy beat me* doesn't excuse the shit he did." My anger is burning hot and I can feel my skin turning red as I huff out the ragged breaths that are supposed to calm me down and stop me from killing the man before me.

"And he was destroyed *because* of her, Avery." His words are dead calm and almost unemotional like my mother didn't matter at all.

"That's not possible because you said it was your father that fucked him up." I am setting now and my fuse is shortening very fast.

"Your grandmother Valerie was married to another man when she gave birth to Lauri, that man was my father. Val was the light of his world only she never loved him, she loved Mick. When Renzo was about four, Valerie ran away with Mick and left Renzo behind. They'd carried on their affair for years, in fact it began before she even married my old man." I don't say anything, I let him continue his story as my assistant brings us coffee and the door creaks closed behind her I feel like I'm in wind tunnel and my world is speeding past me. When I can form a thought, I blurt it out. "But Mick killed Renzo's mother?" The truth is starting to hurt me and I'm not sure I want to hear it at all. "This makes no sense, don't lie to me please. My mother may be gone but I love her, she's my mother don't taint that."

"Valerie never let Mick go, they would meet up and see each other, my father hated that she wouldn't love him. Their marriage was arranged, back then that's how it worked in the mafia families. My father knew that Renzo wasn't his son and it killed him, well the human part of him, a monstrous man was left behind. When Val ran away he became obsessed with finding her, powered by the illusion of love and a broken heart he found them and your mother after nearly two years. She was expecting another child."

"Why did no one ever tell me this?" I can feel tears stinging the corners of my eyes and I pinch the bridge of my nose to try and stop them.

"I don't think anyone knew the whole truth for many years, except maybe Mick." He stands up again now and slides his chair closer to my desk so he can reach my hand, the simple gesture makes this even worse. "Must I go on? This is upsetting you?" I nod, I might as well hear it all now rather than once again learn the truth too late in life. "My father took Val home, forced her to stay with them. He stopped beating Renzo and hit her instead. Renzo believed she was there to save him, but my father had made a bargain with Mick. Lauri could live if Mick killed Val and left Renzo with him. He couldn't have the world knowing his heir and eldest son was a bastard." He hands me a hanky from his breast pocket and I wipe my tears. "The love of a parent is something unique Avery, Mick murdered the only person on earth he loved to save Lauri from being killed or worse. In doing so he sacrificed his love and Renzo, my father hated that boy so much." The man in front of me seems to be just as pained telling this story as I am hearing it. "Renzo was a toxic man, the hatred in him was layered on and built over years and years of abuse. When he learned the truth, that Mick saved Lauri and not him he snapped. She had been free and happy while he lived in hell. She never stood a chance against him."

"I don't want to believe you, because I do not want to feel sorry for him. I hate him so much. Do you know what it's like having no mother in our world?" I snivel past the empty pit in my life where a mother should have been.

"He had no mother or father, Avery, he was broken in ways even I don't understand. He was her brother, that's why he wouldn't let her have babies. He let you live and I think in the end he did love her but it was too late to change who he was. I have no reason to lie to you, they are both dead now. I'm getting what I wanted from the start of this. You should know the truth, all of it, this is your family as much as it is mine. There is always a monster that made the monster and it's usually a much worse one." I let his words sink in, the truth of just how insane Renzo was, the depth of his revenge and hatred was buried under such a deeply disturbing truth.

"Did Callum know all of this?" I wonder just how deep his lies went in my life.

"I believe Renzo told him before he died and left his whole net worth to you. Does it matter if he knew?" There is a knock at the door.

"Go away!" I yell. "To me it matters, there have been many lies woven into my life and it seems most of those were told by Callum, he chose to keep this secret from me and my father." This might have been the truth that healed Rowan, if Callum had told him. Maybe if had a tangible reason for her dying he could have lived, maybe even loved me more.

"What will you do now, Avery?" he asks with genuine concern, perhaps he's scared that I'm going to turn on him, but this madness needs to end so I won't be killing Baldini. I think for a minute before I answer him with a teary smile.

"Make wine and kill people like my father did." I wipe my eyes and nose on a tissue from my top drawer.

"Is that what your heart wants?" What would he know about heart? Then I look at him and I see a monster, but not one like the others I have known in my life. He reminds me of Mathew, a bit of both worlds.

"My heart wants things I will never have." I answer the truth, I am not destined for the things I so desperately long for and I have to accept it and move on with my life.

"Ah, the doctor? He loves you very much. I could tell when he came to me he would do anything in this world for you." He did love me, and as I remember that I am overwhelmed by sadness. I swallow a lump in my throat and try to shake the feeling that I have lost the only love I ever had.

"He did. But monsters aren't always meant to be loved. I'm destined for other things." Baldini lets my hand go and sits back, he looks at me with the sadness of generations of villainous men in his eyes.

"You are wise beyond your years, but let an old monster tell you something, Avery. When you find the person whose demons can dance with your monster, your black hole heart will know it, because there will be no room for anything else. If you can live without them for even a minute then you haven't found the one."

"I can live without anyone. I always have." He smiles and shakes his head at me again, I am not sure why but I like this man more than I should. Our families are sworn enemies for generations yet here he sits with me in an office and there is not an ounce of that hostility between us.

"I hope we can stay friends, Avery, I like you. Perhaps more than my own kids." He puts more coffee in his cup and looks at me like I am a person not like I'm the killer.

"I'm not good with friends." It's the truth I have never had one before, not a real one at any rate.

"Me neither, but I'm willing to try. I think we could be good for each other."

I made a lifelong friend in my office that day, a person that would change the course of my life and be the family I had missed all my life, Baldini was more of a father than my dad and Callum together. I still love my dad, don't mistake this for me not loving him, but I needed more than he could give me and Baldini has plenty to give.

AVERY

Can you actually remove love?
Can it ever be extinguished or forgotten?

WATCHING LUCA BLADINI dismember Callum's empire has been poetic, he has sold the bits off to the highest bidders. Neither of us cared for who bought them, terrorists, criminal individuals, crime families, even governments. We did agree that certain things just weren't worth trading in. People, diamonds and ammunitions are no longer commodities that we sell we have even scaled back the drug operations and the money that has changed hands in selling is enough to see Baldini and his family for generations into the future. He has relocated his family to the Cape, his youngest son is at university here. A few months ago we buried his eldest son after he lost his battle with cancer, I felt his loss as if it was my own because I care deeply for him. He has become my friend and we have even started some uncharacteristic traditions like sharing a weekly meal together at the estate, we drink my wine and eat his food, I did not inherit my mother's cooking skills. With a little guidance from some unlikely heroes, my life has changed and I wake up each day knowing that I have become exactly who I was meant to be.

I used my corrupted political contacts to become part of the solution and not the cause. In a country where criminals are not caught, and when they are the justice system and overflowing prisons cannot make them pay for their crimes there is little hope of eradicating the rot in our society. The government is rich because of crime, but having violent murderers and rapists running free isn't safe. The solution a government funded team that simply removes the problems as they present themselves, I have a purpose. I'm still a killer but now I do it to protect others. My father is probably turning in his grave and I'm sure I have caused Callum to die all over again, but culling the true disease in this place has given me a new life.

I'm setting the table today to have lunch with Luca and some other friends to share some news with them, I got engaged yesterday. Between the vines just outside the little cemetery, the love of my life, the one I cannot live one minute without asked me to share forever with him. We are not the same, but we know the best and worst of each other and still found love in that wreckage. I have suffered all the pain of being attached, and grieved enough to pay for this love a thousand times over and it has been worth it. I can see him walking up the gravel pathway as Jameson charges after his rubber pigeon, we found a bird for him to hunt at the pet store. Our eyes meet and we both smile, he's the consequence of my actions and I'm not even a little sorry for what I have done to get here. My life seems almost normal. I have a dog, friends and a lover, I also have a home that is being renovated and driving me crazy. Strong arms wrap around me from behind as I am lost in my daydreams, soft kisses right in the crook of my neck set the butterflies off in my stomach. My skin prickles with goosebumps and I can feel the rush that his touch causes ripple right through me. "Hello, handsome." I turn around so I can kiss him, he pulls me close his body is hot and sweaty from walking outside in the hot sun. I can smell the signature mix of him and his aftershave. "Are you going to shower before lunch?" I scrunch my nose up and ask him.

"That depends, are you?" I'm so tempted to say yes right there, but it's so late we will definitely get caught by our guests. He grinds his crotch against me, letting me know his intentions weakening my will power a little. He kisses me hard tugging my hair and igniting the lust that I can't ignore whenever he is close to me.

"No, you have got to wait. Owen and Luca will be here any minute." He moans his disappointment into my ear and bites me sending a shiver through my body and making me wish we were not getting guests. There are days I want to kill him, right now I'd like to strangle him for telling them to come over so early!

"You are going to be sorry later, Angel." He smacks my ass on his way into the house. Jameson snarls at him and bares his teeth, the dog really is my best friend. His voice carries as he sings in the shower, it's like nails on a chalk board as it echoes through the empty house. I'm renovating the place. I have gutted the interi-

or of the whole house and we are currently living upstairs in the gym, that and the patio are the only places that haven't been ripped down to bare concrete. I needed to erase the images of my past from this place and make it our home, where the memories aren't tainted and shadowed by the history of those that came before us. The lessons of my past will always be here, they are buried here, but I don't want to live with them in my house forever. The doorbell ring sets the dog off, his cross between a bark and howl is deafening in the empty rooms as he charges for the door like the guard dog he isn't. "Calm down, silly dog." I try to get the door open without him knocking me on my ass. "Hello, beautiful." Owen greets me with a kiss to the cheek and pets the canine as he has a speed wobble darting between us.

"Where's Alex?" he asks as we step out of the mess onto the patio.

"Shower." I answer taking a sip of my coffee that's already cold.

"And you're not in there with him? I'm impressed," Owen says mocking me with his eye roll as the doorbell rings setting Jameson going again and I go to let Luca in. The bell rings again twice before I get there, he has no patience at all.

"Ciao Bella, how are you?" Luca air kisses me and we walk through the cavernous house towards the sunshine of the patio, Owen and him shake hands and greet each other before Luca asks too, "Where's Alex, I thought he's cooking me lunch today?" I giggle, my culinary skills are well known.

"I'm here, you didn't think I'd let her feed you?" his hand on the small of my back reminds me that we are home and I stand on my toes to kiss his cheek.

I lost everything in this world that I had held onto, every small little piece of love was ripped away leaving me alone. When we buried Luca's son something happened, standing in my family's graveyard because Luca's become family. I had let go of love, yet it stood there looking me in the eyes as I held my friend through the grief of losing his child. Mathew was back only he's *Not Mathew*. He never was. The law has changed so he no longer has to hide who he is to do what is right, Dr. Alex Mathews came back into my life. He's seen the worst of me and loves me still. My sweet angel of death.

I look around now at these men and I know I found a family, we are not blood but so much more than that because we have all chosen each other. The empty black hole that was my heart is finally full. We laugh and drink and eat the food that Alex and Owen cook on the grill, the vines are green and the sun is hot, this place is as close to heaven as I have found. Luca toasts us on our engagement with wine from my estate, wine that I named after him. I see Owen and Alex laughing and whispering, men will always be boys at heart, I lost my childhood and have only now found that joy again. After lunch Alex presents me with a box, he is blushing six shades of red as he gives it to me and Owen won't look me in the eyes. I pull the red bow to untie the neatly wrapped gift, no way he did this himself. Lifting the lid I just about spit my wine out all over the table. There is a note and a pink vibrator in the box.

For those days you want to kill me.
XX
I love you

I close the box before Luca can see, I don't want to be the cause of his death by heart attack. I smile so much my cheeks hurt, he really does know me inside and out. And I kiss him before I whisper, "You can try and kill me with it tonight." I wink and we enjoy the rest of the day knowing that the night will be even better.

23022546R00102

Printed in Great Britain
by Amazon